STRANGERS ON NEWBURY STREET

Sarah E Stewart

ISBN: 1517569141
ISBN 13: 9781517569143

For the best mother ever, my mom, "Lizzy"
And for my girls, Delphine, Maggie, and Meredith

TABLE OF CONTENTS

PREFACE

There are people you meet along your journey who touch your life like no one else can. Sometimes you do not realize it in the moment; but later, it is the clearest vision you come to know. They may not linger, you may never encounter them again, but the effect they have is everlasting.

They say the eyes are the window to a person's soul. In all my years working as a therapist, I find this to be quite true. Only in my world, there are four types of eyes: those of a person who would not harm you; the eyes of a person who would kill you in an instant; those who would want you to believe they would kill you, but would not; and then the fourth, the ones we often forget about; hence they can be the scariest eyes you could see. And those eyes, the craziest of all, 'the unpredictable', were the ones staring me in the face.

"Sit down Lexi. We need to talk."

I sat in the chair and my hands squeezed the sides. How is this happening? How did I miss this? That is a gun. A real gun. What have a gotten myself into? I couldn't take my eyes off the gun. Oh my God. I can't fight someone who's crazy.

PART 1

1

THE GOOD OLE DAYS

Walking down the city streets and texting is a skill I would not have imagined mastering ten years ago. And we, the city dwellers, walk down the crowded Boston streets, all of us, walking, talking, texting, rarely looking up. And, yet, somehow, we avoid major collisions with each other, cars, or parking meters. Although I did see a guy do that once; ran smack into a parking meter. I had to turn the other way because I was laughing so hard. It was one of the funniest things I had ever seen. He was ok, just an ego bruise. I still laugh when I think of that.

It's an exceptionally hot June day for Boston. It is as they say a triple H day, hazy, hot and humid. Let's throw in the heat from the car engines and the Sun's rays deflecting off the buildings directly onto the streets and we reach oppressive. Just walking down the street at a slow saunter creates beads of sweat. Everyone is hot, the workers are in white with bandanas; the suits are constantly pulling out handkerchiefs and dabbing their foreheads; we, the city women are scantily clad in linen skirts, tank tops, and big "Jackie O" sunglasses that are never removed because we all know the make-up is just running down our faces. As I head up Mass Ave, every other hand is grasping a sweating bottle of water. I cross over onto Newbury Street and barely manage to bypass the customers lined-up out the door of JP Licks. Ice cream is the number one commodity on a day like today.

I scurry and text, sometimes I look up to check my position. I feel as though I am in a live version of Frogger.

I occasionally glance up and get the usual eyes up and down, the occasional smiles, stares held too long, and a comment from the bold or tactless. I stare back, as if to ask "do you have something you would like to say to me? I dare you." I gain the upper hand; they always look away, chickens. I mean come on, if you are too shy to say hello, please, I would eat you for breakfast. I am not a bitch. I just don't like the snaky guy who stares, thinks he's all that and then backs down. Smile, say hello, is it that difficult? And although I have never truly considered myself exceptionally pretty, I know I am pretty. People stare; friends say I am "hot". I get asked out at Starbucks. But, I am friendly, definitely approachable, and I laugh a lot.

I sound fantastic. I'm not. I am a single 38-year old woman who looks good on the outside and am an absolute disaster on the inside. I can maintain friendships but not relationships. I let people in; but only so far. People expect your life to match their expectations of how you look, and therefore how they think your life should be. I was at a coffee shop once in the middle of nowhere USA, this guy looks me up and down and said, "why isn't there a ring on that finger?" How do you answer that question? I have a list of the top five impossible questions to answer. They are impossible to answer because the people who ask the questions, don't want the truth. They just want to remind you of how you are not living your life up to their expectations.

The number one question on that list: "Don't you want children?" I always feel like my head is going to pop off my shoulders when I hear that question. How is a single woman supposed to answer that? If I say yes then people feel bad and encourage me that someday it will happen. If I say no, then the person asking the question looks at me as though I am some evil monster. I should write a little story-book on "what not to say to single women". Single women everywhere could hand it out to those people who ask such annoying questions. Sorry, I digress often. These are just a few of the thoughts that run through my head as I try to navigate my way through a world where I am clearly not being what others want me to be.

I stand about 5 foot 7, but always wear heals, so a man I would date, must not be less than six feet tall. I have long dirty blonde curly hair that women tell me they love and green eyes. I am thin. I walk a lot, lift occasionally. I love pizza and Mexican food. I smoke and I drink red wine. My motto is everything in moderation. I mean hey, have you seen the way people drive in Boston, I'm not kidding when I say, I could be hit by a bus tomorrow and then wouldn't I regret not having that slice.

So why am I single? I have lots of fake answers like I have focused on my career or I just haven't met the right guy. Yes, I'm afraid of being hurt; but who isn't? The real answer is because I'm a neurotic, control freak who is scared to death of real intimacy. It took me years of therapy processing bad experiences to figure that out. The first of which was my parents dying when I was five. It's hard to admit the truth. I'm so afraid of the person I love being hurt that I will blow up anything with potential before it can destroy them. *I survive and the people I love die.* Although years of therapy has helped me figure out that I am afraid, I haven't exactly gotten to the point of what the hell to do about it. So until I do, I live by the *fake it until I make it* motto.

As I approach the cross walk I stop and wait for the light to change, because although I am care-free at times, I am not suicidal. I look around. The sweat is rather sexy. I space out thinking about sex and how I could really use some in my life. I am impatiently waiting for the damn light to change and I look to my right, directly into the eyes of a stunning man. I mean, wow, stunning. I actually lost my head for a second.

"Hello"

Wow, he even has a great, unexpectedly deep voice.

I pause. "Hi," unsure, "I'm sorry to stare, you looked familiar for a second."

"Really" hot guy replies, "Who do I look like?"

Taking a breath and regaining my composure, the light changes. I walk away from him out onto the crosswalk, turned and said, "I was staring because you're hot! Have a great day."

Back to Frogger, I went, dodging the swarm of people coming at me. I didn't look back but was praying he was following me. Follow me; please be following me, praying in my head. Yeah, my head and me. My head starts to run through all sorts of scenarios. What if he is following me? What if he follows me to the restaurant and says hello, asks for my number? Walk straight, I remind myself, act as if you don't have a care in the world, keep walking, don't turn around, deep breaths and walk straight into the restaurant.

And oh my god did I just say that? Sometimes I can't believe the things that come out of my mouth. I appear confident and occasionally, like now, I say things with confidence. But in reality, I am a total wimp. I don't have any game. If that hot guy was actually following me and wanted to have a conversation, I would fall all over my words like an adolescent boy trying to ask someone out for the prom. Whatever, the man was handsome and I told him so, hopefully I made him feel good. I struggle to get through the Friday evening crowd waiting on the street to get into Stephanie's. I weave through the outdoor tables and into the restaurant bar and there is my crew.

"Hey" I kiss and hug Mike.

"Lex, what is going on?" Mike replies.

"Is there a really handsome man behind me?" I ask.

Mike looks, "Ah, is he tall and dark?"

"Yes!" I screech, eyes widening.

"Then no," Mike replies in his dry, sarcastic way.

"Mike," I whine, "that was mean."

"Yeah, it kind of was, but funny. Did you hear your voice go up like ten octaves?"

"Who are you looking for?" Lindsay and Renee inquire as they both give me a kiss.

"No one" I reply, "just some incredibly hot guy I may have complimented."

"Nice ballsy ass move Lex!" Mike states as he holds up his hand for a quick high five.

"Hey, I am too old to not tell a hot guy he is hot right?" I ask as I slap Mike's hand.

"Absolutely", my brilliant friends chime together.

"Miss," the hostess gently grabs hold of my elbow, "your table is ready."

"Great, thank you." I turn to Mike, "let's rally the troops.

"I'm on it." Mike replies, as the two of us head to gather the other members of our crew, who are scattered throughout the bar.

As Lindsay, Renee, and I make our way toward our table, they asked many questions about the mystery hot guy but I waved them off. I have learned over the years that I need to wait on story details until everyone is gathered together so I only have to tell the story once.

So at our large table we sit, all seven of us. Yes, seven of us, most of us have known each other for years. Typically, our group numbers 15, however, not everyone could make this evening's soiree. We met in college, one by one, sometimes two or three at a time, and now, 18 years later we all still are the best of friends. It is truly remarkable and we are lucky. Some of us have left New England, came back, some still working to get back, and some never left. We have lived through marriages, deaths, births, and well, the marriage that never happened. That would be mine. It was not one of my stellar moments, telling my fiancé I couldn't go through with it on the eve of our wedding night.

Sitting down to my left is Renee, one of the three women whom I truly love like a sister. Renee is beautiful. Well, all my friends are actually. Of course I say that because they are my friends. Everyone is rather intelligent and successful. You never would have guessed that during our glory days of college. But Renee is beautiful, smart, and has a fabulous, outgoing personality. She is married to Alina, a woman who now, is starting to tolerate us. Ah, yes, Renee is a lesbian. Again, something we probably would not have predicted in college. Many men are drowning themselves in beer trying to figure that one out. Ha, about time the tables are turned. Women do it every day. We find that wonderful guy, who is so handsome, and fun, and loving, and, yeah, gay. Renee and Alina have two beautiful children. (Yet, another thing my friends have done remarkably well, procreate). They just moved back here from Dallas, TX. I'm not so sure Alina is all that happy about the move, but she's coming around.

Next to Renee is Zoe, another sister. Zoe is just a riot. Very little seems to phase Zoe, and you never know what will come out of her mouth. We were once standing at a bar and a rather rotund man tried to push his way through us to make his way to the bar. Two of us spilled our drinks with his push. The rotund man just looked at us and laughed, stepped up to the bar and ordered a light beer. Zoe turned to him and said, "Yeah, keep kidding yourself with the light beer."

Zoe, too, is a beauty. She is about 5 '9, dark hair, brown eyes and the best complexion you have ever seen. Zoe actually grew up in the Boston area, and yes, at times her accent can be quite strong. We all say you have to have some thick skin to be friends with Zoe, because like or it or not, she'll say it. She'll tell you, you are too chubby, too thin, you have wrinkles, or ask with a disgusted look on her face, "Did you really buy those cheap shoes?" Now, as much as she can dish it out and she can take it as well. And most importantly, she has your back!

Zoe is married to Sean, the love of her life. Yes, that's actually a young crush story that came true. They too are married with three beautiful kids. Sean is a guy's guy. He is solid, wonderful and adores Zoe. He runs his own business and might I add, quite well. He certainly is a risk taker and sometimes that works out well, sometimes, there are very stressful weeks. All in all, they are just fine.

Lindsay is my third sister. She is a wonderful and an amazing friend. I met her one night as she was sitting outside our dorm smoking a butt. I remember it was so cold out and since I smoked, I told her that my door was always unlocked, and to feel free to smoke in my room. We've been best buds ever since. Lindsay is married to Mike. They met when they were 18 and fell in love. They have been together for almost twenty years. If I could find what they have, I wouldn't let it go. They are both my best friends and have seen me through thick and thin.

"Okay, tell us the story," Zoe chimes, half whining.

"What story?" I reply.

"Lexi, hot guy, tell us."

"There really isn't that much to tell. I was rushing here, walking, and texting. And then, there he was and he took my breath away. He looked a bit like that English actor, Hugh Grant. I think I was only staring for five seconds, but I'm sure it felt like eternity. So, I apologized, lied and said I thought I knew him and he called me out on it."

"Did he have an English accent?" Renee asks excitedly.

"No. I think if he did I would have melted into the side-walk."

"What did he say?" Zoe whines a lot when she is curious.

"He said, 'really, who do I remind you of' and I was thinking shit, totally busted, and then as luck would have it the light changed, I walked across the street, turned half way and told him he did not remind me of any one I knew, I just thought he was really handsome."

"Yeah, and then she walks in here all deer in the headlights asking if some hot guy is following her, and of course I said, oh is he tall and dark."

"You're an ass Mike, but funny" comments Alina.

"Just how hot was he Lex?" asks Renee.

"I can't explain it. He just had a presence, a very unassuming presence. Maybe that was part of his allure. That's what made him appear to be so stunning." I reply.

"As stunning… as Ty…???" Lindsay asks rather coyly.

I laugh; Ty is my best city friend, my best guy friend, my best single friend, my realtor, and the hottest man you have ever seen. You know how some people have their celebrity crush, as far as looks are concerned, well, mine is not a celebrity, he's one of my dearest friends.

"Please, he was stunning, not fall down on your knees stunning, but whatever, random guy on the street." I wave my hand to dismiss the conversation.

"Oh, please…" cries Zoe, "Random guy on the street, like random guy at Starbucks who asks you out or random guy at the car dealership who asks you out, or random men at the trade show who ask you out. Shall I keep going? You OWN random guy."

As I smile big, and laugh. "That is true, I have had a few random guy moments, but look, do you see him, no, I do not have his number, and he does not have mine, this random guy, although hot, really random. But, damn, if I ever wanted a Lexi random guy moment, this would be it. Besides, he's probably married or a player."

"Did you actually just say that? "Asks Renee.

"Oh my God, I did. Man, I sounded like an old bitchy chick. Huh? I hope I am not getting jaded."

Sean chimes in "you know Lex, what's up with that anyway. Why is it that women think if a guy isn't married at a certain age, there is something wrong with him or he's a player?"

"Sean," I begin my reply, "first of all, that is a loaded question. And secondly, women don't think ALL men of a certain age are players, just the HOT men. And are we feeling a little self-conscious. Protecting your peeps or your former reputation? Sean, you were a player in college, you're married now, and you're good."

"Well then what is the difference? Wouldn't men see you as a player Lexi? You're hot, single, 38. You date all the time, why is he potentially a player and not you?" Mike asks.

The girls all start together, jumping to my defense, "hey, Lexi is not a player, please."

"All right," I start, 'look the difference is a player does not want the commitment but will say he does OR she. They will do whatever it takes to get the hottie in front of them right now. Certainly, I have had my share of dates and relationships, but I am not looking for right now, I mean ultimately, if I met the right person, I would settle in."

"R-e-a-l-l-y," Sean says in this loud, I-am-so-calling-you-out-tone-of-voice, "Really, Lexi? You would settle down? Miss I don't even book my travel arrangements until the night before. You can't even commit to a hotel room. And do we even need to bring up the little "run-away bride" incident?"

"Hey!" I reply with a big ole smile on my face, you have to laugh when you are being called out. I also have to laugh so that I don't burst into tears. It's not easy having your fears thrown in your face. "First, we have all long since agreed, running away was the right thing to do. And technically, I did not run, I told him straight up, to his face…"

"Yeah, Mike interrupts, then you friggin' sprinted across the country for four years."

"True, again, we have all agreed, that too was a good move. And yes, so I am a little gun shy on the commitment front. However, I don't intentionally seek out one-night stands or flavors of the month. I want to, you know, be with someone, in a relationship…thing. And how did we get from hot guy on the street, to my complete fear of commitment?"

"Lexi," Renee comes to my rescue in her sweet tone of voice, "we are just bored in our little suburban lives and need to vicariously live through yours."

"You mean my screw ups?"

"No, your exciting mini life events."

"Well, enough about random guy moments and my life events." I say as I raise my glass, and the table quickly follows suit, "Here is to all of us! Happy Saturday Night."

Nick was happy to head inside the bar and get out of the hot steamy Boston air.

"Nick, over here buddy!"

"Richard, hi, so good to see you man." The two men shake hands, and do the quick guy style pat on the back hug as if they were burping each other.

"How long has it been?"

"Too long." Richard replies.

"So what are you doing in Boston?"

"Well, just here to check on a few things before heading off to Europe. I thought, damn, I have got to call Nick, and as luck would have it you were free and here we are. So how are you? How's your life, work, women, tell me? I am a married man Nick; I need to feed off your bachelor lifestyle."

Nick smiles, a long drawn out, spacey smile, "good, everything is just fine."

"Whoa, wait a second, everything is just fine, are you kidding? That is not the Nick Jacobs I know. Who is she?"

Nick hung his head and smiled. "I don't know actually."

"What?" Richard asks loudly.

"You're never going to believe this but I swear I just saw the woman of my dreams and she basically told me I was hot."

"What?" Richard, shaking his head, waving to the bartender, "two beers please." Richard pauses, looks at Nick's faraway look, "and two shots please!" He turns back to Nick, "What?"

"Dude, I know, it's unexpected. I was walking over here and then this woman was staring at me while we were waiting for the light and she apologized and said I looked familiar, so I asked who I looked like, the light changed and she just walked away."

"She just walked away?" Richard asks in disbelief.

"Well, then she made it half way across the street and she turned and told me I didn't look like anyone, she thought I was handsome, and to have a good day."

"So did you get her number?"

"No."

"What, why not?"

"I was thrown off by her confidence I guess, I'm not sure. I'll say this, I'm intrigued."

"Well, why didn't you just follow her and ask her for her number? I mean come on, you're Nick, you are not new to this game dear sir. It's actually your forte."

Nick shakes his head. "I don't know. I just don't know. God I'm such an idiot. I mean I do this stuff all the time. I have interrupted board meetings to get a number. I must be coming down with something. No big deal, there are plenty of hotties out there. Hey, enough about me. What big case are you working on in Europe?"

Richard grins. "You know I can't give away my secrets Nick."

"All right then, how long are you in town for?"

"Let's just say that is yet to be determined." Richard coyly responds. "I can't discuss that either. I wanted to say hello and see you."

"You mean before you disappear into the crowd and take on a persona of someone I have never met?"

"Exactly." Richard appreciates the long friendship he has with Nick. They have an understanding and trust that has been tested by time. Richard needed to let Nick know he was in town. Boston is a small city and Richard can't risk the off chance that Nick recognizes him while he is blending into the crowd.

"So how are Sally and the kids?"

"Great. You know, for the most part we live a happy little life. I always wonder when Sally is going to get sick of me jetting off to work on yet another case, but she doesn't."

"Well, she knew what she was getting into when she married you."

"She did. I am a lucky man Nick. So how about you? Aside from this mystery woman, how is work? Any chance that Seattle project will come through?"

"Every year, they say they want to open the Seattle office and every year it doesn't happen. I think I might start looking at other options soon."

"You could always come work for me."

"Richard that would be great. Except, I don't know what the hell you do."

Richard laughs a hearty laugh. "Good point."

Nick finds it intriguing that he has known Richard since college but he's still a mystery. He looks like the same old Richard. He probably stands a good inch shorter than Nick and has slighter build.

His hair is gone and he has a little gut that he jokes comes with love and happiness. He is a good man and a good friend. He would go unnoticed in any crowd. His appearance is unremarkable; yet, he is completely mysterious. Nick pushes a shot glass toward Richard. Both men raise their shot glasses in the air and Nick says, "Well my friend, here is to your exciting life, I wish you safety and success."

"Thank you, although, rest assured I am never the one in danger." Richard clinks Nick's glass and they down their shots. "Listen, I have to run, give me a fifteen-minute head start." With that Richard throws forty dollars on the bar and heads out the door.

"Take care." Nick says as he watches his friend exit on to Newbury Street. He shakes his head as he finishes his beer. Nick has never really been sure if Richard is a private investigator or a hit man. *Richard has a wife and two young children; he could never hurt anyone; he's a P.I.* Nick assures himself.

After an insanely decadent meal and perhaps a few too many drinks, my friends and I stream out of Stephanie's and say our good nights. The sun has gone down but the air is still warm and heavy. I saunter down Newbury Street in the opposite direction of my friends keeping my eyes peeled in hopes of a very lucky second chance siting of the random hot guy.

Newbury Street is still quite busy with late evening shoppers and fellow diners. I continue my vigilant crowd scanning and the weirdest thing happened. I suddenly felt cold. It's hard to explain. It was like the moment slowed down exponentially. I looked up and passed someone. I didn't know who he was. But it felt like I was moving in slow motion. Have you ever seen a puff of smoke hanging in the air while the sun shines on it? It's mystical. The smoke just lingers, and looks like it slows down as it passes through the sunshine. When you watch it, you know that time is moving at the same pace it always moves, but the smoke is dissipating so slowly it feels like time itself has slowed down. That is what it was like, time slowed. We passed each other and stared, and for a brief second we locked eyes.

"Oh, sorry about that." Said some person who bummed into me.

It snapped me out of my slow motion time warp. I stood there for a minute and looked around. The stranger was gone. I looked around again, slightly panicked but everyone seemed normal. Everyone was going about their evening activities. I didn't know him, but something was weird. I couldn't explain it. Something was off, the way he looked at me, and it was unsettling. I decided that the vodka tonics were getting to me and I headed home. I walked quickly though as I just couldn't shake the creepy feeling I had.

2

When I first moved back to Boston from Los Angeles, I was very fortunate to find a fantastic apartment on Beacon Street in the Back Bay. I was so lucky to move here. It is a 10 -story building with about 67 units. The building is all condos and is majority owner occupied. I have met some wonderful people. I needed that. I needed to be in the middle of everything when I moved back, little did I know, not only would I be in the middle of Boston, but also I would be in the middle of all of these wonderful people. Young, old, students, professionals, different races, different religions, different countries, all of us just having fun and finding our way in Boston.

The downside of all of this fabulousness; I live in 450 square feet. I have two rooms and a very tiny bathroom that consists of a toilet, pedestal sink, and a shower stall. It is tight; but Boston isn't cheap. I get all of this for the very low price of $2300.00 per month. I was paying $300.00 per month for parking as well; but I needed to cut costs so I had to forgo the luxury of my own little private parking spot next to a dumpster. Oh the joys of single city life.

One of my favorite new things to do since moving to Boston is to sit out on the stoop, soak up the sun, sip on coffee, smoke a cigarette, and watch. I watch the crazy Boston drivers, blaring their horns if the light turns green and the person in front of them isn't instantaneously hitting the gas. I laugh as the people run down the street, texting and talking on the phone with the funny things in their ears. And yet, I'm right here, as is everyone else, what is all the panic about? We are all right where we should be, aren't we? Where is everyone going? And why are they always in a rush?

Those are just some of the odd questions that pop into my head when I am alone and observing others. Of course, when I am really busy or running late I think very differently. For instance, when I am trying to race up Newbury Street, dodging all of the shoppers who always manage to walk really slowly and take up the entire sidewalk. You know whom I'm talking about. They walk three or four across and stop suddenly, for no apparent reason, and finish a conversation blocking the entire sidewalk. You almost have to have magical powers to get around them. In that moment thoughts come to my mind like, "why are you shopping and not working? Get to work." Or when I am standing behind someone at a coffee shop at 7:30 in the morning and they just can't seem to decide what they want. I think, "why are you not sure what you want to drink? If you are at a coffee shop at 7:30 in the morning, you should know what the hell you want."

Ultimately I like this time the best, just relaxing, by myself. I cherish it actually.

I have spent the last seven years of my life traveling constantly. The work that I was doing kept me flying from place to place and spending about 275 nights per year in hotel rooms. I was always on the go. It's refreshing to sit here on my stoop and not be one of those people racing to get somewhere.

Being on the road all of the time means my life looks very different from that of most people. I don't have a gym membership or drinks with the same people every Tuesday. It means that I probably don't know all of my neighbors but if you are going to a city you have never been to, I can make some great recommendations on where to eat. It means that my Facebook page is filled with pictures of places not people. I have enough airline miles to fly for free anywhere in the world and stay on hotel points for a month at a five-star resort; but I would be doing it alone.

Alone and on the road was something I was very tired of being. I decided to make changes in my life. And after years of planning, these changes are finally about to come to fruition. This week is the beginning of a very big shift in my life. If I'm honest, I will tell you that I am scared shitless about it.

My phone beeps snapping me out of my philosophical thought process. It is from a man named Patrick, with whom I have a date tonight. It reads:

> *Hi Lexi, looking forward to seeing you tonight. I appreciate you squeezing me into your busy schedule. How about Sonsie at 9 p.m?*
> *I text a reply: Great, see you there.*

A date, I haven't been on a date in months. What am I getting myself into?

"So, I have since tried to put Random hot guy out of my head, rather unsuccessfully. I mean seriously, Boston is one of the smallest cities on the planet. I always run into people, especially those I don't really want to run into. How is it that I see the most amazing man, in my own neighborhood and three and a half weeks later, no sign of him. How is that possible?"

"Well," Renee replies, "it could be because you travel constantly and have only been home six days in the last three and a half weeks. Or, maybe he wasn't from here."

"True, I'm going to go with 'it is my travel schedule', because at least that still leaves the slightest, tiniest possibility that I could run into him again. I am not a big fan of the he's not from here scenario"

'So who are you seeing tonight?'

"I don't know, this guy named Patrick."

"Patrick, that's a nice name."

"Yeah right, shocking a guy in Boston named Patrick, but get this, his last name is Fitzpatrick!"

"You're joking?"

"Nope I have a date with Patrick Fitzpatrick."

"That's hilarious! But oh the boys will just tease you incessantly if this date turns into anything. Where did you meet him?"

"Trust me, I've considered that fact. My friend John had an impromptu gathering last week at Tapeo on Newbury Street. I met him there. We chatted; he seemed cool enough, although a little odd. He had this weird staring thing. I'd ask him a question and he would just stare for a bit and then answer it. I don't know that much about him and to be quite honest with you, I thought he was gay. Needless to say, I was rather surprised when he called and asked me out."

Renee laughs. "Okay, but he sounds a little frightening. Is it safe to go out with him?"

"Um, I think so."

"So are you interested in him?"

"I don't know. I think I'm bored. I haven't been on a date in a really long time. And well, come September, I'm not going to have time for anything."

"True. Did you put your usual rules in place?"

"But of course, darling. I have a 'late meeting' tonight so I couldn't possibly do dinner and a very early morning conference call; however, would love to have one drink."

"Well, have fun, baby cakes, call me in the morning."

"Will do. Kisses"

I hung up the phone with Renee. 8:15p.m, hmm, I'm meeting Patrick at nine, about a ten-minute walk from my house, perfect, just enough time to run downstairs, smoke a butt, and ponder my exit strategy. I'm really not that cynical about dating. I mean it's necessary. And most of the time, I am completely up for it. It gets you out and I have met a few nice people along the way. Some of whom, I'm actually still very good friends with. And I need that. I mean I love my core group of friends, but they have different lives than I. I also need people my own age to hang out with who are in the same boat as me. And, surprisingly, there are a lot of us out there. Just some nights, honestly, I am tired. Curling up with a glass of red wine and mindless television is so much more appealing than going out and trying to be charming to a perfect stranger. Whatever, I grab a cigarette and head downstairs. (I smoke, but never in my house, or car, I mean really, it is a disgusting habit).

It's a beautiful evening. It was a hot July day, but a huge thunderstorm rolled through and cooled everything off, which also means it is a great hair night. The streets are wet but the air was dry. I inhaled my cigarette, blowing it out, I pictured random hot guy. Then I laughed to myself. I could not quite figure out, why, after four weeks, I am still thinking about him. It is not really my style, I mean, I travel everywhere, and I see plenty of handsome men, why is he stuck in my head? Do not misunderstand me; I am not obsessive. All week long, I really don't have time to focus on anything but the people in front of me. But as I am about to go out on a date, he pops into my head; I guess there is that little wish that I could be having a drink with him. All right, so I'm busted. For all of my objective, realistic traits, there is a part of me that is a complete romantic. I take my last drag, roll my eyes at myself, toss my butt in the butt can (which I think is there just for me), and head back upstairs to get pretty.

My outfit for the evening consists of casual jeans, a cool scoop neck tee-shirt, a short black light casual blazer and of course, some very cute, sexy heels. I am going for the casually sexy look, and avoiding the let's jump into bed crazy look. I step out of my apartment, head downstairs, out the building doors, and off I go up Beacon Street to Mass Ave. As I turn the corner onto Mass Ave, I decide not to cross the street because the light is still green, I will catch the next cross at Marlborough. As I was waiting for the light to change, I am standing on the edge of the side walk when all of the sudden this cab comes flying up the street, and right in front of me, a huge puddle. Shit, I turn quickly but don't quite get out of the way fast enough. I arch my back as I am getting splashed and yell, "Shit!!" I hang my head and laugh in defeat.

And then I hear a snicker, "Are you all right?"

I lift my head, and holy shit, random hot guy. And then, I look left, random, YOUNG, BEAUTIFUL, hot chick. Without losing a second or one ounce of composure, I say, "Yeah, just a little wet."

Being 38 I know a thing or two about human behavior so I quickly look at young hot chick, turn my back to her and over my shoulder ask her, "How bad is it?"

She brushes my back and responds, "no, you're good, just water, no dirt."

I spin around to face both of them and simply reply, "nice."

In an instant young hot chick is sprinting to the street hailing a cab, she turns and yells, "Thanks for dinner Nick!" And blows him a kiss.

Nick responds with a wave and, "You're welcome Chelsea." He turns to me, "so, hi"

"Hi. She's cute." I respond trying to hide my utter disappointment.

"Chelsea, yeah she's great. I'm Nick by the way," he says as he extends his hand.

"Pleasure to meet you Nick, I'm Lexi." We hold our shake a bit too long and man does he have nice, strong, big hands.

"So Lexi, you forgot to tell me your name last time we crossed paths."

Thank you universe, he remembered, and uh oh, I can feel the blood rushing to my face, why do I blush so easily, I quickly hang my head and laugh. "Yes, well, you know, busy intersection, I was just throwing out a compliment, you didn't need to know my name."

"Is that something you do often? Tell strange men they are handsome?"

"Often, is kind of a relative term don't you think. No."

"Well, then, I'm doubly flattered." He held eye contact almost to the point where I was uncomfortable. He is tall probably about 6"1', thick dark hair and eyes that are the coolest green color. His skin is tan and he is wearing jeans with a casual white button down, my favorite outfit.

"Well, Nick, I'm glad to hear that, I'm actually running a bit late." I say as I point my finger up the street. He was just with a gorgeous young woman. As handsome as he may be I need to move on from this conversation to avoid any further heartache.

"Big date?" he asks.

"Hmm, I would not call it big, but yes, I am meeting someone for a drink." I emphasize the A. What the hell is my problem why am I flirting with this man?

"Ah, not sure on this one huh? A drink not dinner."

"Well, let's just say, I have learned along the way, dinner can be a rather torturous first date."

Nick laughs. "But, don't you think just drinks can be misleading?"

"No, not when you stress the fact that you only have time for one drink because you have a very early meeting in the morning."

"Ah, I see. But what if you like the guy and want to have more than one drink?"

"Well, that is the situation where everyone wins. You have already set a limit, so you have an easy exit. No one is hurt because you have clearly stated you only can meet for one drink. However, if you are interested and having fun, then you say, well, I can stay for one more. Everyone is happy, he knows you are enjoying his company, but you still need to leave after the second. You know, I have a bunch of guy friends who have adopted this line as well. It can work both ways."

"So, when do you actually decide you want to have dinner with someone?"

"I don't have a steadfast rule, if all goes well, I can usually tell, if someone seems interesting enough to get through an entire meal."

"Huh." Nick ponders my answer, "So, what are you doing tomorrow?"

"I have dinner plans actually."

Nick's eyes widened with surprise, "Really?"

"Yes, with my friends, in the burbs." Shit why did I just say that? I have absolutely no game.

"Oh, cool." he says as he quickly calms down. "So, how about Saturday?"

"I don't have plans on Saturday."

"Well, then Lexi, how about dinner?"

"Well, wouldn't Chelsea have an issue with that?"

"Chelsea? No, I don't think my cousin cares what I do."

I half smiled, thinking nice brazen play. "Dinner works." I say without missing a beat.

"Great, dinner on Saturday. May I get your number?"

"Sure." I say coolly, all the while my body was ready to burst with excitement.

We exchange numbers and say a rather awkward goodnight, as we both know I am off to meet another man for a date.

Now typically I don't smoke before a date. I mean I do, but then I go upstairs and brush my teeth and change my clothes et cetera. But, really, can you blame me? I just ran into random hot guy, who now has a name, and with whom I now have a date, all while on my way to a date with another man. And this is why you must date; you just never know where the night will take you.

I light a cigarette. Anyone passing by me would have thought I was on drugs. There is a spring in my step and the biggest smile on my face. REALLY, OMG, did that just friggin' happen. I take a drag, slow my pace, and I exhale. I need to focus. Patrick, I am meeting Patrick. Shit, poor Patrick, not a chance in hell. What do I do? What do I say? My mind was racing. I turn onto Newbury Street and I am about two blocks from the bar where I am meeting Patrick, I put out my butt, toss it in the sidewalk trashcan, and throw a handful of mints in my mouth. Still trying to figure out how to handle my little dilemma, I swing open the door to Sonsie, pass by the hostess, give her a head nod and veer towards the bar.

Sonsie was an interesting choice for a first date. It is always a great night out, but usually with friends. It has good food, but is consistently packed. It hosts an interesting mix of young people, people my age, and older people. It is a great place to people watch, but a first date, I am not so sure. Maybe I am off the hook. Maybe Patrick was thinking, *hell one drink might as well go to a place where I can continue to socialize.*

As I gaze through the crowd of people standing in the bar area, I see a person who looks like Patrick from behind sitting at the bar with an empty seat next to him. I make my way and lo and behold it is Patrick.

"Hey Patrick, so sorry I am late. How did you get these seats?"

"Lexi, hi. I know, I was lucky, right as I got here this couple left. I pounced. So how are you? Nice to see you again." Patrick stands up and pulls out my barstool, leans over and gives me the standard, kiss-on-the-cheek greeting.

We do the usual awkward chatter as we both sit and adjust our bar stools, slightly turning them toward each other. The bartender makes her way over and we have to quickly order considering how jammed the bar is this maybe the only time we see her. Patrick motions towards me, "What will the lady be drinking tonight?" he asks, half smiling at his own formal line.

"Ah, I'll have a Ketel One Citroen and tonic with a lime please."

"Interesting choice" states Patrick, "I will have a Ketel One Citroen and soda with a lemon, thank you."

Patrick turns back towards me as the bartender heads off to make our drinks, he says, "Well, it has been my experience Lexi that people are all or nothing when it comes to tonic and soda. Let's hope we can find some common ground in other things since we certainly won't find any in how we drink our vodka."

Our drinks come quickly and Patrick just hands the bartender his card to start a tab. *Wishful thinking buddy, I already established the one drink rule,* I think to myself.

Patrick raises his glass to me, "Cheers, thanks for meeting me, it is really nice to see you again."

"Cheers, and thank you." I respond as we clink and sip.

I have learned over the years, how to take a compliment and just accept it. I tend to be a people pleaser who always needs to make people happy. It has not been an easy experience to learn to just say thank you and not give into my intense desire to respond in kind.

"So, "Patrick starts, "John tells me that you are starting a chocolate business here or something?"

"Yes, I am. I'm taking a huge leap, completely leaving my field and hopefully turning my avocation into a lucrative vocation. To be determined."

Patrick looks at me rather intently. He is staring again. He has great brown eyes with very full eyebrows, not crazy bushy, just perfectly full. With a big excited smile on his face he pushes the inquiry. "Tell, me more about this huge and very exciting venture. Do you have a location? How far along are you in the process? What kind of chocolate business are we talking about?"

I smile half blushing, "Well, I guess I can give you the short synopsis, otherwise we will be here all night with me doing all the talking."

Patrick sits back in his stool, "Look you are the one with the early conference call, I wouldn't have one issue with sitting here looking at you all night and listening to what you have to say."

It has been said that I can be a bit sarcastic. There are times, like this one, where I should let stuff go, but, then, often, in times like this, I just can't resist. "And there it is, the first cheesy line of the night. And only ten minutes in, love it." I hold up my glass to give Patrick an opportunity to take it like a man and clink. He accepts with his head down, laughing.

"Oh, man, John warned me you were tough Lexi."

"I know, I'm sorry, I couldn't resist, you threw me a softball. I mean really, what option did I have?"

Patrick still had his head hung, laughing. I started to feel badly, so I reach over put my hand on his knee and half whining, "Oh, Patrick, I'm sorry. I was totally just messing with you."

Patrick looks up at me with a huge smile on his face and says, "And I didn't even have to pout too long before I got the sympathy touch."

I lean back, pulling my hand away, "Ah, and let the games begin."

Patrick raises his glass, "touché."

I go on to tell Patrick the very brief summary about my business venture. It turns out that he is a Sloan MBA who started a computer software company with one of his fellow graduates. Patrick works the sales side of things so he tends to travel quite a bit. And although he is three years younger than I, you would never know it. He is strong, handsome, experienced, smart, and well, as it turns out, quite witty. Who knew? We actually had a lot to talk about. Our drinks sat empty for thirty minutes, without either one of us really noticing until the bartender came over to ask if we wanted another round.

"Well, Miss Lexi, I know you have an early morning, but can I persuade you?"

"Actually Patrick, normally, I would say yes, but, I really need to be sharp tomorrow, so I am going to have to pass this time."

Patrick motions to the bartender for the tab and turns to me. "Well, I would like to have a chat with whoever scheduled such an early call on a Friday morning, but, be that as it may, I'm glad I got to spend some time with you."

I smiled. Patrick signed off on the tab and we made our way through the swarm of people who had gathered around us eyeing our seats. We walked out onto Newbury Street and I turned to Patrick to thank him for a fun evening, but before I begin Patrick nods his head towards the direction of Mass Ave, "Come on," he says, "I'll walk you home."

"Patrick, you live in the South End, there's no need to do that, besides, it's hard to catch a cab by my house."

Patrick gives me a whatever look. "Lexi, If you don't want me to walk you home, because you don't want me to know exactly where you live, let me assure you I'm not a stalker. Let's go."

I turn and start walking, thinking two things, first it is always the ones who claim they aren't stalkers, who are. Second I really like the chivalry. I'm such a sucker for that.

We stroll down Mass Ave and the conversation continues to flow as easily as it did when we were sitting at the bar. We arrive at the corner of Mass Ave and Beacon Street, one block from my building and I turn to him, "Ok, I live right down there, but, this is the best spot to catch a cab."

Patrick laughs, "Ok, Miss Lexi, I will accept that compromise. I would really like to see you again."

I thoughtfully nod, "Sounds good, you have my number and thank you for the drink. I had a great time."

Patrick stood there for a second staring, hands in his pockets, he shrugs his shoulders and said "Yeah, you're going to have to walk away because I could just stand here and look at you all night."

I smile, "Well all right, talk with you soon." I turn and start walking.

I was about halfway down my block I turn to see if he was still there, and he was, same pose, hands in his pockets, just watching. I shake my head and keep walking. Although, I don't want to cross the street. I don't want him to know exactly where I live. He seems nice but my gut is telling me to be safe. I duck into the entryway of the building directly across the street from mine. I slowly count to sixty and then poke my head out. He is gone. I cross the street and head to my favorite smoking spot in front of my building. As I pull out a cigarette I realize I have a big ole smile on my face. Apparently I like the uncertainty of whether or not he is trustworthy.

3

THE SIGNING

My alarm sounded at the insanely awful hour of 5:30 in the morning. I am not a morning person. One of the things I miss about Los Angeles, there isn't a lot going on early in the morning. The East Coast is full of early birds, which is tough to take some times. But today is a huge day. Although I didn't have a very early conference call like I initially told Patrick, I did have a meeting with my realtor Ty, at 7:30 a.m. We are set to go over any final details and then at 8:30 we are meeting with my new landlord to sign the lease for my retail space. Today marks the beginning of what I hope will be an exciting new venture in my life. For the last 15 years I have worked as a therapist. I have dedicated my life to helping others. And although very rewarding, it was also very draining.

Over the last eight years, I have carved out a rather unique and lucrative consulting practice. It really wasn't anything I was looking for; it all just fell into place. Early in my career, worked as a therapist in the prison system, and then I began working on a project that helped the families of inmates. From that point I started to do some crisis work with families of the accused or convicted. This area really piqued my interest and I became quite good at it. This population is one that is often forgotten about; however, still deals with a large amount of trauma, even more so when it is a high profile crime. My name just started to get out in the field and the next thing I knew, I was flying all over the country to work with various families, through their shock, trauma and grief. I must say, there are some shocking stories. I mean, how would you feel if you woke up one day and found out your father was a serial rapist, or your husband just bilked millions of dollars from investors and your luxury life is all a lie. The calls came from everywhere and everyone, family members, friends, judges, prosecuting attorneys, defense attorneys, anyone really. Sometimes I would be with the family for a day, sometimes weeks, and occasionally, multiple visits over a few years depending on how long the trials would last.

That is actually how I ended up in Los Angeles in the first place. I had, as my friends tease, run away from a potential marriage, and just kept running. I was dealing with a few cases in the LA area at the time so I figured, why not. I could use a change of scenery for a while. Of course little did I know how life-changing Los Angeles would become for me. It's still something I cannot speak about, not even to my friends. The wound runs deep, but I know I have to talk about it. I can't keep walking around with my little secret. I guess, right now, I just want things to be as normal as possible. So hey, let's start a business. When I was younger I thought chaos just found me, at 38, I'm starting to think I might have something to do with the chaos.

I became a little fried in Los Angeles, both personally and professionally. The intensity of my work can be overwhelming. You do become a bit hard to it. You don't become callous, but you compartmentalize. You have to. You can't possibly listen to everyone's trauma and not learn how to shut off the emotions when your day is done. Unfortunately, I started to get to the point where I could no longer compartmentalize. I started to cry more frequently, not sleep well and obsess about whatever case I was working on. When those things start happening that is when you know you need a break. Couple this with the terrifying event that I personally experienced in Los Angeles and well, not only did I need to stop the work I was doing, I needed to leave LA. I was hoping if I ran from LA, I would run from the emotions as well. It worked for a bit, but now the emotions of what happened there are catching up to me. I'm always paranoid and looking over my shoulder. Ugh, stop thinking Lexi.

I do still consult, I have cases that are not complete, but I am not currently taking on any new cases. Instead I am focusing all of my efforts on chocolate, happy, little, drama-free chocolates.

You learn a few key things in the early stages of your career as a therapist. You learn that you will not always know all of the answers. Someone or a few will probably die on your watch. People will want you to have one of two things, a magic wand or a crystal ball. You will have neither. And you learn that you need a hobby, one that is not stressful, but gives you the satisfaction of completing something. You need to see a finished product, hopefully in a short amount of time. I chose truffles.

I remember the first attempt at making chocolate truffles. My roommate and I had both recently completed graduate school, she a teacher and I a social worker for the Department of Social Services. Not exactly the most lucrative careers. We were both not only living paycheck to paycheck, but day to day. At the holidays we decided to be creative and make gifts. I'm not exactly sure whose idea it was to make chocolate truffles, but we did it together and what a disaster! We actually bought marshmallows and caramels, unwrapped them, and dipped them in chocolate. We even attempted chocolate coated, brandy soaked cherries, more than likely using maraschino cherries, awful! However, we did find one thing that worked, Bailey's Irish Cream truffles. After that discovery, I started to expand my chocolate horizons. I even made my own marshmallow and my own caramel. It worked. I got to the point where I was making about 1500 truffles every holiday season and actually had pre-orders. Everyone, for years, told me to start doing this for a living. I always had it in the back of my head, just never really got around to taking the leap.

Chocolate was my hobby but it was also my release. As a therapist, you are often working with people who are very sad, angry, or in crisis. Therapy is a process so you don't see results right away. Chocolate became my way of doing some work and creating a finished product. It was also my tool to instantly put a smile on someone's face. Something you can't always do in therapy.

And now, full circle, here I am. It is the morning of the lease signing for the actual retail space on Newbury Street, one of the hottest addresses in Boston. What the hell am I doing?

I jump out of bed and start the coffee; I take a brief look out of my kitchen window to see the rowers out along the Charles. Crazy group, rowers, they are early risers, out and about exercising. My morning exercise consists of walking to the kitchen, scooping out the coffee, walking to the bathroom and showering. That's about all I can take for morning exercise. It's a total of about twenty steps. My apartment is very small. I must say however; I do have one of the best views in the city. I have a corner, ninth floor apartment. One side overlooks the Charles River, and yes, I have seen some amazing sunsets! One window in my living room frames the famous Citgo sign, while the others pan across the Back Bay encompassing the Prudential building and the John Hancock. Most days, not a bad view to wake up to! And on this particular morning, I am feeling pretty darn good about Boston. Today is July 24th, 2015; hopefully it will be a memorable day in my life.

I pour some coffee and head to my couch, still admiring the grand view that I don't think I will ever be sick of. I flip on the news and drone out for a bit. My thoughts drift to a vision of Patrick, hands in his pockets, looking all innocent and cute. Whoa, wait, Patrick? Really? Huh. Again, interesting. Random hot guy has a name, and I have a date with Sir Nick, but yet, I can't get over the surprise fun and cuteness of Patrick. Then my thoughts jump to the stranger I saw on Newbury Street. Who was he? That was a very odd interaction. I'm not even sure I would call it an interaction. I'm not sure what to call it.

The weather guy snaps me out of my trance, 80 degrees, sunny, and dry is the forecast for today. I jump to my feet and head to the bathroom for my hair straightening ritual. Yes, I am told by so many they love my curly blonde hair. I'm not so sure they would love it on a humid or rainy day when the curls tend to get all frantic and crazy and I look like a blonde medusa. Another bonus to living in Southern California, perpetually great hair days. I blow dry, straighten, and throw on a bit of makeup. I'm not really good at the makeup thing, I always feel as though I'm a little kid playing dress up.

I head down stairs with a fresh cup of coffee to smoke my morning butt. This is usually when I feel the most guilt about smoking, in the morning. Especially, since my stoop is on Beacon Street and rather busy sidewalk for those early morning runners and walkers. Whatever, I'm over it. To each her own.

I head back upstairs, leave on my jeans and throw on a cute short-sleeve white button down. I laugh as I walk into my closet to grab some heels and see all of the suits I will no longer have to wear. That is certainly going to be one huge benefit of the new business, I get to wear my favorite, jeans and shirts, and my dry-cleaning bill will go down exponentially! Yahoo!

I head up Beacon Street, with my purse or city satchel as I like to call it, loaded down, with paper work, check book, identification et cetera. It is funny in July; the Back Bay is exceptionally quiet. The summer time is slow throughout the entire city; however, Back Bay tends to have a significant slowdown without all of the college students in town.

As a 30-something living in a City like Boston that is known for its academics, its population significantly increases with the influx of college kids, you tend to have a love-hate relationship with the college kids. I love their energy, their playfulness, their awkwardness, and their fashion sense, or lack thereof. I certainly feel much more comfortable when they are in town, especially when walking home at night. You can always count on tons of kids being out and about in the late hours of the evening, which will give you that safety-in-numbers feel. What I hate, well, the usual, listening to the yelling, screaming and sometimes, yes even throwing up at one in the morning on a random Wednesday. Oy Vey! Overall, I think the ever-changing waves of college kids coming in and out of Boston, are pretty damn cool. And hey, I am certainly going to be banking on those kids to need some serious chocolate fixes during their academic years. Did I say cool, I meant to say I love them!

I turn on to Newbury Street from Mass Ave, easily cross over Newbury Street, not too many people are on shopping streets at this early hour. I fling open the door next to Starbucks and scan the room for Ty. All of the sudden I feel a hand circle around my waist from behind, and the most sultry voice whisper, "Ready for your big day?" Of course, all of that didn't register in the moment, instead it scared the shit out of me and I jumped about four feet and spun around.

"Jesus, Ty, don't do that to me! You know, I'm NOT a morning person!"

Ty just stepped back, bent over, and laughing. Still laughing, Ty reaches towards me to give me a hug, "ah, come here, baby girl, you know I'm just messing with you." He wraps his arms around me and I give him a playful open handed smack in the chest.

"All right, grab a seat and I will get you... um... decaf?" Ty asks.

"Hell, no." I reply, "high test, it is barley 7:35 in the morning."

I head over to grab a table while Ty, still smiling, waits in line. I sit and watch. He is one of the most handsome men on the planet. I actually met Ty when I was still living in Los Angeles. I had been in Austin Texas, of all places, working with a rather high profile family whose patriarch had just been indicted on federal charges of embezzlement. The family was from Houston, but because of their status and the publicity of the case, they preferred to meet with me in Austin. They would fly me out from LA, two times per month; put me up at the same over the top glamorous hotel and our sessions would take place in their private suite. I often wondered how they could afford all of it, along with my fee, considering the circumstances, but that wasn't really what I was there for.

Anyway, one night I flew to Texas and there was a National Realtor Conference going on at our usual hotel. The bar was packed and I was starving. I squeezed myself into an empty seat next to this rather sketchy Texas dude and this amazingly handsome black man, who turned out to be Ty.

Ty and I started talking while drinking and eating and just hit it off. He stands about 6 foot 2, perfect body, amazing dresser, big round, brown eyes, that make you melt and in case you don't melt, well, his smile will do you in. To top it all off, he's nice, smart, and funny. So, as we sat there, two, potentially single, attractive people, drinking, eating laughing, why did we never hook up? Well, turns out, Ty was in the middle of a rather difficult divorce. And of course, me being me, I don't know why but people tell me stuff. Ty told me lots of details that night. With that said, divorce or any big break up for that matter, is always my biggest red flag.

I have this saying, some people like it, some people hate it, some shake their heads in complete agreement: "your head doesn't come out of your ass until two years post." Again, it could be a divorce; it could be a long-term serious relationship. Now, I'm not saying you can't date during those two years, I'm just saying, as an informed consumer; I'm not going to date you during those years.

You actually should date, you need to date, for some, you need to learn how to date. It is just that your emotions are on an amazing roller coaster ride. One minute you crave and desperately miss that sense of knowing someone, the regular conversations, the day-to-day interaction (the stuff that you seemingly got bored with in your marriage or serious relationship). Then, as you get closer to the person you are dating, and that stuff you were craving and missed so desperately starts to appear, you freak out and run. Again, these are all normal reactions. I just happen to know them because, well, I've been the one going through it, I've been dating the person going through it, and I've watched many friends and clients go through it. It is a painful process to watch, it is an excruciating process to go through. Personally, I'd rather be the one watching and supporting as best I can.

Now, some people do get through the process sooner, some longer, but my best estimate is two years. So if I meet someone and they are somewhere in that process, I do not date them. And I especially don't date someone who is just starting the process, as was Ty when I met him.

So there we were, Ty and I, sitting belly-up at the beautiful hotel bar in Austin Texas. Me, a New England girl living in LA. And he a born and bred Boston man, living in Boston, and selling real estate. As it turned out, Ty was winning some big national super star award. He really wasn't into the award at the time, and as he said, he never would have gone to such a thing except that it seemed like a good idea to get away from Boston, considering his personal circumstances. I love meeting fellow fleers, even if just for a brief evening.

We really connected that evening, and I'm not going to lie to you, Ty could have been talking about why certain types of grass grow better than others, and I would have had a great evening. But we connected on a more emotional level. It was as if, we both knew, even though, there may have been an attraction, nothing was going to happen between us. It took the pressure off and we were just able to be ourselves.

The night ended with me having to leave because I was facing a rather intense day of therapy with my clients. Ty and I exchanged information with the hopes of seeing each other again, especially with my connection to Boston. We've been best friends ever since.

I say Ty is my "realtor". He actually owns one of the most prominent real estate agencies in the Back Bay. He usually doesn't waste his time with little projects like a lease signing. But, Ty is my guy, he's always there when I need him and he is taking care of this minor transaction, more to take care of me than anything else. Someone has to hold my hand when I turn pale and start to shake as I sign a lease for an outrageous amount of money. *Oh, God, what am I doing?*

"Hey, baby girl," Ty sits down and slides a coffee across the table to me, "get that cold feet stare off your face this instant. You may run away from men, but you're not running away from this. This is your dream Lexi." Ty reaches across the table and grabs my hand, "Listen to me, I'm your biggest fan. I've had to run a lot of extra miles since I've become so addicted to your truffles. Lexi, this is going to work."

It's true; Ty has become one of my biggest fans. He even started ordering my truffles last Christmas to give as gifts for his employees and clients. His employees and clients were among the first true strangers to have my chocolate and they were all after him as to where they could buy the "stuff". One night over dinner and a bottle of wine, well actually, it might have been two bottles; Ty and I decided that I should start the truffle business. He helped me with my business plan, and we just sat back and waited for the right spot to come open, and here it is.

"Remember Lexi, 'better than sex' and I quote." Ty teases as he sits back with a big grin on his face.

"Yeah, you know Ty, I still feel bad for that guy who thought my chocolate was better than sex, I mean really, what's better than sex? Speaking of which how was your date last night?"

Ty rolls his eyes, "B-O-R-I-N-G! Lexi, thank god you taught me the one-drink rule or I would have contemplated offing myself in the men's room."

I laughed, "Ty, don't tell a therapist you were considering 'offing' yourself."

Ty just kind of gazed at me with this half smile, like he was somewhere else. "Ty?"

"Hmm, yes, and do tell, how was your date last night?" Ty responds, coming back to earth.

"Actually, it was nice. I mean I really enjoyed his company. But the kicker, Ty, I ran into Random Hot Guy, who, now has a name, Nick. And, I have a date with him on Saturday."

"What?" Ty's eyes are all wide as he leans in closer for the good gossip.

I proceed to tell Ty the events of the evening prior. He was astounded by my random luck.

"Why can't that happen to me Lexi? Why does this lucky stuff always happen to you?"

"Um, well, first of all, have you ever told a woman you just happened to pass on the street and find incredibly beautiful that she is? I mean let's start there." I say as I give myself a pat on the back with my own words.

"Touché" Ty replies, "All right, you ready to head out?"

"Yeah, and Ty, thank you for this."

"Baby girl, again, free chocolate anytime I want. Thank you!"

Ty and I head out of the coffee shop, both donning our sunglasses to avoid the early morning glare as we head up Newbury Street to his office. As I walk down the street and see all of the shops preparing for the day, I forget about the fact that I'm about to sign a lease worth a gazillion dollars and my nervous stomach gets a hint of excitement for what is ahead of me. My shop, my business, here in Boston, on Newbury Street, holy shit!

The signing of the lease went off without a hitch, which really means, I was able to keep my hand steady enough to sign on the dotted line. The lease doesn't begin until September and my business is not scheduled to open its doors until October, which is ideal, just in time for the colder weather and the Holidays.

I kiss Ty goodbye and check in about our dinner plans for Sunday night. Ty and I have a great little weekly ritual of Sunday dinner. We either go out, order in, or one of us cooks, we re-hash our crazy work-weeks, and our even crazier weekend events. It is such a great segue from one week to the next. Unless I am on a plane, we are both very dedicated to those Sunday nights. Although we laugh about the time when we will actually have to break our ritual if either one of us starts dating someone seriously. But, we have decided to cross that bridge when we get to it, until then, they are our sacred Sunday nights and I have come to heavily rely on them.

I walk out the door of Ty's office back onto Newbury Street. The summer Friday has begun. The traffic is getting heavier and the sidewalks are filling up with pedestrians. I decide to head down to the Esplanade and continue my walk home by the Charles. I'm guessing once September comes, I'm not going to have a whole heck of a lot of time for detours.

My mind is racing. Although this plan has been moving forward since January, I still can't believe it is actually going to happen. I'm not sure whether to get sick, cry, or start jumping for joy. I have done so many things along the way. I've taken my food safety classes, completed my LLC, met with lawyers, and health inspectors, builders, and advertising agencies. I have completed so many steps; however, signing the lease and actually having the space, makes it so much more real. Holy shit. I think that is going to be my phrase of the day.

I stroll along Dartmouth Street and find my way down to the esplanade and plant myself on one of the docks along the Charles River. I zone out watching the sailing classes out on the river. It's really rather humorous. The sailing lessons are unruly. They put about ten boats out on the river and then there is someone in a motorboat with a megaphone screaming instructions. How there is not some huge boating accident is beyond me. All I see are kids laughing and scrambling as they tact from one direction to the other, barely missing another boat. I'm sure there is a method to this madness, but from here it just looks like a disaster waiting to happen. And then, there is that one boat that seems to float away from all of the madness. It happens every time. The kids on that boat usually have a confused look as the boat sails in the opposite direction of the crazy circle. The instructor occasionally looks back and gives them a yell to turn the boat around. And the kids are trying, but they can't really figure it out. Eventually the instructor has to go and get them and tow them back to the mayhem. Then, twenty minutes later, there they are, floating away from the sailing circle of hell. I can't say I blame them. If I were in that class that's where my boat would be going, away from the chaos.

Sometimes that is how I feel about my life. I feel as though I'm sitting in that boat, watching all of my friends in the circle; traditional jobs, marriage, children and all of the tacking, laughing, and near misses that go along with that circle. At times, it looks like fun and sometimes I join in, but then, I don't know, I get scared, or the circle gets too small and frantic, and I have to wander off.

I take a deep breath and hop to my feet. That's enough self-reflection for one day. I need to get back to work. I meander slowly along the Charles as I have no desire to get to work however, I have to as I have paperwork to do and invoices to send out. Spending more money than you are taking in is not a good feeling.

As I am nearing the Mass Ave Bridge I can see the bridge is full with lunchtime pedestrian traffic, runners, bikers, and walkers all crossing between Cambridge and Boston. I look up and see to the left a large group of runners about to head down the ramp that I need to walk up. I step aside and look up to my right. Up on the bridge there is a man standing there looking at me. Holy shit it's him! He is wearing the same trench coat and cap. It's the man I saw as I was leaving Stephanie's. He sees me looking and then quickly turns away. I step to enter the ramp and am practically plowed over by runners. Shit.

The last runners blow by me and I clumsily run up the ramp. My high-heeled shoes were clearly the wrong choice today. I make it to the top and look to my left and to my right. There's no sign of him. He's gone. *Who the hell is he?* I lean back against the rail of the bridge. *Am I going crazy? I'm just stressed. I just signed a lease for a lot of money and I am settling in. It's stress. I need to get to work and get back in control.*

I jump about three feet when I hear, "beep beep". Yes, we all know that sound, whatever it is on your phone, the sound that lets us know a text message has arrived. It's amazing how that sound can seemingly rule my life. It makes me happy, fills me with dread, or like right now, scares the hell out of me when I least expect it.

I look at my phone and am pleasantly surprised to see a text from Nick. *Ok take a deep breath Lexi and do a reality check. Do you want to read this text from a man you have been pining for, for over a month or do you want to focus on the creepy stranger who may or may not be totally made up in your head?* I'm going to opt for Nick.

"Hey Lexi, are you busy or may I call?"

Okay that man just scored huge points! I am all about the texting thing. I live in a city, sometimes when you are walking down the street it is much easier to text then try and speak with someone while cars are honking their horns, sirens sounding, et cetera. I appreciate texting when on a plane; as a matter of fact, I wish more people would love it as well. I can't tell you how sick I am of this conversation:

The plane is about to take off. Random passenger on the phone: "Hi, yes, we are just about to take off. What, No, we are just about to take off. I will call when we land."

The plane lands. Random passenger gets on the phone again, "Hi, yes. Hi, it's me. Yes we just landed. We are taxing to the gate. Yes. I will call you when we get to the gate." You get the picture. For someone who flies all the time, may I suggest texting?

I also love texting when working out details, or texting among friends, or just a random sexy text when you know your lover is in the middle of a meeting. I'm fine with all of that. What I hate are the people who have now replaced speaking in person with texting. Have we all lost our social skills? I once had a guy ask me out for the first time via text. Needless to say, I never responded. In this case, I respond to Nick:

I'm free.

Two seconds later, my phone rings and I answer, "Hi there."

"Well, tell me Lexi, what does a beautiful woman do with herself on a sunny and warm Friday such as this?"

Before I go any further, I have to say two things. First, years ago, I may have deflected that comment by saying something self-depreciating like, "well, I'm not sure, I guess you'd have to ask a beautiful woman." But, again, that is such a lame thing to do. It doesn't show any self-confidence, it makes you appear as though you are looking for more compliments, and probably doesn't give the person who made the statement a very good vibe. Secondly, and, at this moment, and much more importantly, this man has the most amazing voice on the planet! I know I mentioned, when I first met him, that he had a great voice, but I don't think I actually gave it full credence. You know what his voice does? It instantly turns you on. To the point where you don't care what is behind the voice, lights off and just keep talking!

"Well, right now she might be on her way home from the Charles, just trying to take in the sun before she heads back to her work."

Nick laughs, "Oh, I'm jealous! Well, I do hope you are enjoying yourself. And even more, I hope we are still on for tomorrow night?"

"Absolutely," I respond.

"How do you feel about Sushi?" Nick asks.

I laugh to myself. I hate fish; I don't even like the smell of fish. I pause, trying to think about how I break the news. "Well, honestly Nick, I'm not a big fan, I hate fish."

"What?" Nick gasps through the phone. "You don't like fish?"

"Yeah, no, sorry."

"Ok, well, how about margaritas, do you like margaritas?"

"Oh Nick, you are working your way towards scoring a hat trick of things I can't even pretend to like."

Nick was silent for a second.

"Nick?"

"Yeah, I'm here, I'm just trying to make sure I don't score that hat trick. Hmm, tell you what, I'm going to take you to a place that has a little bit of everything. That way, I can observe and learn about what is in and out in Lexi's world."

"Sounds like a plan."

"Great how about if I pick you up at eight tomorrow night?"

"Perfect. 534 Beacon Street, just call me when you are close and I will meet you out front."

"Done." Nick confirms.

"Great I'll see..." I stop as my phone screen flashed. I look at my phone and realize he just hung up. That was odd.

I put my phone away thinking I'm breaking lots of rules here. I mean, I'm having dinner with him on the first date, and he's picking me up! That is also a rule I have. I tend to just meet people on location versus having to be in a car with them, especially early on. It could be my control issues, perhaps, a little safety thing, or a combination of both. Whatever, it should be an interesting evening, and besides, it's RANDOM HOT GUY!!! I mean Nick.

I get a little giddy and check the time. Shit, it is 12:30 already. I push myself off the bridge rail and head towards my apartment. I have so many things to do before I head to Suburbia.

4

SUBURBIA

When I arrived home I had to do a quick shift from the excitement of my future business to the monotonous tasks of my current one. I do love the work of consulting and connecting with people, and of course, get satisfaction from the thought that I may be helping someone. Again, as I mentioned, I'm just fried from it. I am fried from the work and the travel. I log into my email and see 50 un-read messages. As I begin to scan through my unread messages I see one from a defense attorney in Dallas, Texas.

Dear Lexi,

I received your contact information from Detective Davis with the Dallas PD. It is my understanding that you may be leaving the field. I was hoping you would consider taking on one last case. The case involves a young man here in Dallas who was arrested last week for multiple accounts of rape and murder. The parents of this young man are well respected in the community and well, to say that they are in shock and extremely distraught would be the understatement of the year. You can access more details about the case through the links I have provided below.

Thank you in advance for your consideration.

I push my chair back from my desk and hang my head. I don't need to read the details. I can only imagine how much pain and distress these parents are feeling. I have done this for so many years. I have sat with families through investigations and trials. I have worked with them to try and get them through the crisis, handle the media, and tolerate the horrific onslaught of hate mail. I have watched them be alienated by lifelong friends, lose jobs, and be ousted from their community. I have watched people lose everything and age ten years in a blink of an eye all because a relative committed a crime. I wish I could help them but I no longer have the emotional strength to handle their pain. I return to my laptop and send an email to the attorney respectfully declining the case and provide a list of names of others who are well suited to do the work.

By three in the afternoon my work is done and I am getting a little sleepy from writing client reports. I also realize that I have to leave shortly to head to Suburbia, so I throw on a small pot of java, wrap up the last details and text Zoe to see if she needs me to pick anything up. Yes, I am that girl, not the *what can I make girl*, the *what can I pick up girl*.

Zoe responds,

Z: "just wine."

L: "White or red?"

Z: "Lindsay is making a red sangria."

L: "How about both?"

Z: "Sounds good."

I pour myself a cup of coffee and head downstairs to smoke a butt before I jump in my car. *Uh-oh,* I think to myself, *Lindsay is making Sangria, this could be an interesting night.* I walk outside and plop my coffee cup on the cement wall that lines the stairs going down to my building. It is a perfect smoking perch. Just as I am about to hoist myself up on the cement wall, I get a cold feeling. It sends a chill down my spine. I walk up the steps and look up and down Beacon

Street. Nothing, just cars and a few pedestrians. No one looked odd or creepy. Maybe I am getting sick.

Tonight, or I should say, this afternoon because it is four thirty in the afternoon, I am heading to Zoe's for a little Friday evening Soiree in Suburbia. It's something that happens often but I only attend every once in a while. Zoe and Sean's home is about twenty minutes south of the city and is a great place to gather especially with the number of children my group of friends have. The problem for me, is that it's twenty minutes south of the City. Friday night, summer time, the traffic is brutal! Yeah, the famous Big Dig really didn't seem to do much to relieve the congestion, it just stuck the congestion underground. Between the usual Friday evening traffic, and all of those heading to Cape Cod, the drive will actually take me over an hour.

I pull into Zoe and Sean's driveway, already seeing Lindsay and Renee's cars parked, the kids running around the yard, and right behind me Sean pulls in and then Mike. We all jump out of our cars to a mass of kids running at us screaming "Daddy" and "Lexi!" It certainly is an amazing moment. The unconditional love that I get from these children who are not even my own, is rather cool. They just attack you and are so happy to see you, albeit, a brief moment because then they rush back to the same exact point in the yard from which they came. Like a swarm of bees surrounding Sean, Mike and me, they flew in, chaos ensued and then they flew away.

I give Sean and Mike a kiss and we all walk into the house. I put the wine down on the counter and in the kitchen sit Lindsay, Renee, and Alina, while Zoe does her thing around the stove. All with a glass of Sangria within reach.

"Hey ladies," I begin, "So um, the kids asked if they could just take a walk up the street and we all told them to go ahead, that's ok right?"

I was joking of course; Zoe and Sean live on a very curvy, rather dangerous for walking kind of street. I just couldn't miss the opportunity to make a mockery of the fact that the moms were all in the kitchen, drinking, while the kids, randomly played outside unattended. Of course, no one flinched, because they didn't believe me, except for Lindsay for a fleeting moment, which leads me to believe she might be on her second glass.

In keeping with the routine of these Friday evenings, the kids are all fed first, usually chicken tenders and a salad. They are herded in, the dining room becomes like an elementary school lunchroom and two seconds later they are done. That's another cool thing about these kids, they are fast when they are hungry. And off they all go to watch a movie about two rooms over, (so we can't really hear them unless there is a scream), and chill out for the evening. It's a sight, all seven kids, on the floor, in a room, a bunch of arms, legs, and pillows, wide-eyed; and all entranced by the "magic of Disney".

Then of course come the adults, chatting and drinking in the kitchen, as Zoe prepares some amazing meal (all the while making it look really easy). Zoe is a fabulous cook. I keep telling her if my chocolate shop works maybe she would consider working with me on an expansion and providing "real" food.

Next thing I know, Zoe is lining the counter with seven champagne glasses and pulling a rather expensive bottle of bubbly out of the refrigerator.

"Well, well," I say in my snootiest voice, "what is the occasion?"

"YOU!" Zoe replies like I should have known, "You're the occasion, you did sign the lease today right?"

I could feel my eyes filling up with water, not shedding, but filling, and the lump forming in my throat. It is so unexpected and of course, my friends are always there to celebrate triumphs, and ice the lumps. I hate being the center of attention. It is this weird paradox within myself. I mean I am very outgoing. I don't have any issues with public speaking; I actually quite enjoy it. But being the center of attention in this fashion, just throws me off. Perhaps it is my deep fear of failure. I like to do things on the QT and let people know if I succeeded or failed after I already have. This wonderful celebration, where my friends are proud of me and are publicly demonstrating their pride, brings me right to the *Oh God, what if I fail, what if I let them down* moment.

Zoe catches a glimpse of my eyes and stopped pouring, "Lexi, you did sign the lease right?"

"Yes," I snap to. "I did, I guess, I just got so caught up with my other work this afternoon that I forgot. Yes, this is a good thing. We should absolutely celebrate how much debt I am going to be in!"

Zoe continues to pour as everyone laughs and grabs a glass.

Sean begins with a toast, "Ah, dear Lexi, there's nothing like the rush of having your fate in your own hands. The energy that will come with your day to day sales and the agony you will feel while trying to balance your books at the end of the month, and asking yourself 'where did all of the money go?' No sir, nothing like it." We all clink.

And there he is again, Sean to the rescue. In his very brief statement, acknowledging all of the anxiety, excitement, and day-to-day success, which even still might not add up to an overall win. He runs a business he gets it. Sometimes my friends, as wonderful and as intelligent as they are, don't really understand how difficult this process is. Sometimes they think along the lines of "build it and they will come." I wish it were that simple. They also compare the success of my consulting practice to the potential with my chocolate business. What? Not even close. The consulting fell into my lap. And yes, eventually I took the leap and left my secure, steady pay check, but not until I had built up quite a nest egg and had more cases than I could handle. That was actually one of the most secure job changes I had ever made. Plus, this is me; this is what I do for fun. The chocolate is almost an extension of me. My nightmare is actually seeing someone taking a bite and watching the look on their face turn to disgust as they spit out the chocolate into a napkin. It would feel as if they are disgusted with me and spitting me out.

"Thanks Sean, and you will all still love me and love my chocolate even if the retail shop fails, right?" I raise my eyebrows as I seek out their reassurance.

"Please, Lexi, it's not going to fail, it will be great. Your truffles are awesome." Lindsay states in her reassuring yet don't be ridiculous kind of way. Had I asked her how do you know, she would've said, "because I know." And that is the gospel of Lindsay. It is the trait you love to hate and hate to love depending on whether she is defending your honor or dismissing your idea.

"Yeah, Lexi" Renee jumps in, "you can't go into your business thinking it is going to fail."

"Okay, hold on." I put my hands up to stop the attack of support. "I am not going into this business thinking it will fail. However, I am faced with the reality that these things do fail. And, I would be an idiot not to consider that fact."

"Yes, but Lexi, you could be creating a self-fulfilling prophecy if you go in thinking the negative and that you will fail, and actually do." Renee protests.

"I'm not thinking it is going to fail. Again, just considering the realities, and if you would all let me finish, perhaps you will understand my side. It's a fact, that these businesses have a high failure rate. One must always consider the facts. What I did was two things. I started with making a list. I tried to imagine myself sitting in my apartment after the business had failed, and I made a list of all of the things I 'wished' I had done, but did not."

"But, how can you make that list if you don't know?" Mike asked.

"Well, it is based on guessing and assumptions, but what I can tell you is, I had better be doing, proactively, as I begin my business, everything that is on that list. If I don't well then yes, to Renee's point, that would be a self-fulfilling prophecy. Now, I also realize, Mike to your point, my list is a guess. So the second thing I did, with the help of friends and a little research, I contacted some people who did have a small business fail and I asked them, what they wished they would have done, or had done sooner. I got some responses that were on my list and some great things that were not."

"But Lexi, what about asking people why they succeeded versus why they failed, I mean isn't that what you want to know." Renee says still beating her positive drum.

"Of course, but there's a whole section in Barnes and Nobel on that perspective, that's the easy stuff to find, when people win, they want to tell you."

"Those are excellent points Lexi," Sean understanding all I am saying, "I mean, more people should do that before they take the leap."

"Absolutely Sean. And those words were said to me. One guy actually said, 'I wish I would have done what you are doing right now.' And of course there were a lot of people who said, the timing was off, the location, wishing they had more financial reserves and one that really hits home for me, due to my control freak nature, they wished they had enlisted the help of others sooner."

"Well, we are all here to support you, especially when it comes to taste testing the goods!" Mike states as he leans back and sticks his belly out as he rubs it. The irony, Mike, who stands about 5'11" and is thin, can stick his belly out further than anyone I know. It's too funny.

"Speaking of eating," Zoe replies, "let's eat, it's ready."

We all sit down at the large wooden dining room table, set off from the sitting area, in the most French Country decorated room on this side of the Atlantic. The food is fantastic, the company even better and the conversation flows more and more crazily as the sangria and wine start to disappear. I have stuck with my usual one drink limit due to the fact that I am driving. I'm adamant about that. It's just wrong. I always do have a toothbrush and sweats in my car just in case I feel like crashing on Zoe and Sean's quite comfortable couch, or I break my limit.

It's interesting to remain sober, watch and listen to the conversation slide rapidly downhill and digress into old arguments and old habits. It's as if we are a family of siblings. Nothing is sacred or off limits and if liquor is involved, well, you know how that goes.

It is consistent, Zoe will give Renee and/or I shit about our lack of weight, and that my ass is flat. She may comment on someone's fake leather shoes or fake leather bag. We will all harass Sean about his latest metro-sexual hairstyle. Lindsay will give us a lecture on how hard she works. Sometimes we give Zoe a hard time about how good she has it, she doesn't work and yet her house is always a complete disaster. Mike varies; he is either breaking the tension with his humor or causing tension by going after Lindsay. If he goes after Lindsay about some issue they have been bringing up for the last 20 years, we all tend to give him a hard time. Alina tends to get by unless she is wearing something Zoe absolutely hates, then she gets its. At times she gets a little possessive about Renee, when she does it in front of us, we call her out on it. All in all, just good fun, and typically the night ends, or goes on forever, with lots of dancing (or so we would like to call it) in Zoe's kitchen. Definitely not a place to bring someone I have just started dating, unless I want them to run away screaming.

"Wait a second," Lindsay stops the conversation as if she has just solved the global warming crisis, "Lexi, didn't you have a DATE last night?"

"Hey, that's right," Renee joins in, "you were supposed to call me about that today."

"Time to fess up Lexi, and don't spare ANY details." Zoe insists.

Sean rubs his hands together, "Let's hear it."

"Wow," I reply, "Such a Lexi focused night. It was nice. Patrick is his name and yeah, he turned out to be a really cool guy. And I have a date tomorrow night." I reply coyly.

"With the same dude?" Asks Mike.

"Wait," Zoe interrupts, "Wait, first, what happened last night, then we'll know who she is going out with tomorrow."

"Nothing 'happened', I had one drink, I mean I really didn't even have to lie, I did have an early meeting that was pretty significant in my world. We hung out, I totally forgot about random hot guy, whose name is actually, Nick, and Patrick walked me to the corner of Beacon and Mass Ave and that was it, no kiss, nothing. But he did say he wants to see me again, and I may go out with him." Now, I casually named random hot guy to see if anyone noticed, or caught on. Also, a good test of just how drunk everyone is, because sober, the girls would not miss a beat.

Mike blew my experiment, "Wait, who's random hot guy, and who's Nick? I thought you went out with Patrick?"

"I know Mike, single life man, it's hard to keep up" Sean commiserates.

I almost see the light bulb go off in Renee's head as her eyes widen, "WHAT? How do you know his name is NICK????"

I proceed to tell every one of the events the evening prior and how I met Nick. And tell them about the date I have with Nick tomorrow night. Lindsay insists on knowing where we are going so she and the girls can be a fly on the wall and check this "dude" out.

"I don't know where we are going, he is picking me up at 8:00."

"Wait, Lexi, you don't know this guy and you're getting in a car with him? Are you crazy?" Zoe replies.

"Well, no, I'll just leave ONE of you with his number and if something happens to me, you know who to go after. You guys, I'm going to dinner. I will text you the minute we get to the restaurant so you all know where I am."

"And the minute you get home." Renee demands.

"Well, no guarantees on that one." I slyly respond.

"Lexi" all the girls chime in together.

"Kidding, easy, down girls. I promise."

The evening, or shall we say the crew, starts to progress to sloppy, which is when I decide it is time to head home. I get the usual protests but, again, sloppy so the protests are never strong or lasting. I grab my things and take a quick glance at my phone and see I have two missed calls and two new text messages. I'm startled to see they are all from Detective Moore from the LAPD. Detective Moore is someone I worked very closely with on a number of cases in Los Angeles.

Detective Moore: Lexi. Please call me.

Detective Moore: Lexi, this is very important. RE: AM. Call me please.

I read the last text and gasp. I feel my eyes fill with water; I inhale and hold my breath to try to keep my composure. I blink my eyes a few times to get the water out of them and turn to say my good-byes.

Renee takes one look at me, "Lexi, are you all right?"

"Yes." I say as I let out a deep breath at the same time. "I'm fine. It was just an emotional text message from an old client. It's nothing."

"You sure?"

"I'm sure. Thanks."

I kiss all good-bye and head out the door. I cried the entire way home.

5

MY SECOND FIRST DATE

I didn't sleep a wink last night. I tossed and turned and my mind was racing. I lay awake in bed and feel as though I'm going to crawl out of my skin. I will myself to get out of bed. I need to go for a run. I need to get this anxiety that is pulsating through my veins out of my body. I throw on some running clothes and head out onto Beacon Street.

As I head towards the Charles River running path I take note on what a beautiful morning it is. The sky is bright blue and the air is dry. I walk down the Mass Ave bridge ramp to the running path. Even though it is only seven in the morning the path is already full of walkers and runners. I convince myself to start running. It's more like a slow jog, trot kind of thing, versus a run. As faster runners pass me by I try to quell my competitive tendencies by reminding myself I am not racing, just clearing my head. I see a couple of women pushing baby strollers while they run. I decide they will be the ones I will compete with and try to pass. Although, I shouldn't fool myself, if a woman is running, while pushing a baby stroller, she's not kidding, she's a kick ass runner. I finally pass the first stroller pusher; it takes me longer than expected but I feel accomplished. As I near a small incline, I hear something behind me, all of the sudden that baby stroller pushing, kick ass-running woman, passes me. Now that is humbling. Whatever, I can make truffles. I don't actually yell that, but believe me, I am thinking it.

I get home with a slightly bruised ego and take a long shower. I was hoping my jog would snap me out of my sullen mood. It hasn't. It's a gorgeous sunny Saturday and I should be outside soaking up the sun. I know I shouldn't be sunbathing. People are constantly saying that to me. Things like, "Wow, you have such a great tan, but, oh, the damage the sun will do." But, honestly, there are two things people should know before they judge me. First, I don't wear anything less than 30 SPF. Secondly, feeling the heat of the sun is just so incredibly relaxing to me. Everyone has their sacred relaxing thing, baths, tea, manicures, pedicures, or massages. For me, it is being half-naked, in the open air and feeling the warmth of the sun on my body; it is heaven. Besides, I grew up in the era before the whole "protect your skin" was so well advertised. Hence, the damage is done, can you say, baby oil on a black tar roof, my teenage years!

Even the thought of the warm summer sun doesn't make me rise from my horizontal position on my couch. I stare at my phone. I know what I need to do but I can't quite get myself to do it. I know I need to call Detective Moore, but I can't. I don't want to talk about Ashley's case. I can't bear to hear anything else. I miss her so very much.

My phone begins to vibrate. I look and see that I have the all too predictable texts, one after the other, from Renee and Lindsay reading, "agh, I wish I left when you did, rough morning." I laugh to myself while reading the texts, just the comic relief I need. A phone call comes in and I see it is Detective Moore.

"Shit," I say aloud as my thumb hovers over the decline button.

"Detective Moore, good morning."

"Lexi, good morning, how are you?"

"I am well, thank you. I'm sorry I didn't call you last evening I was with friends and not in a place where I could have a conversation."

"That's fine Lexi. How is Boston by the way, are you ready to come home yet?"

I grin. "This is my home remember?"

"Yeah, but really Lexi, you're a Californian at heart. We miss you."

"Check back with me in January, Detective, then I may be singing a different tune."

Detective Moore laughs. "Yeah, I don't know how you deal with those winters. So Lexi, is everything okay? Are you doing okay?"

"Yes, fine. Why?"

"Well, Lexi, I'm not sure. We had some lawyer calling here and inquiring about Ashley's case."

I gasped into the phone. "It's not..."

Detective Moore interrupts me before I could finish the question he knew I was going to ask. "No, no, not a defense attorney. He was a lawyer for some financial firm. He said he just wanted to ask some questions. My concern Lexi was that all of his questions were about you and your relationship with Ashley."

"Me? Why me? Ashley and I didn't have any financial ties."

"That's what I told him. It's probably nothing Lexi. I am sure he is just covering all of his bases. They believe there were some things of value in her apartment and they seem to have gone missing."

"But, I never stepped foot in her apartment after..." I couldn't say the words.

"I know Lexi. We assured him that no one stepped foot in her apartment except for the investigative team and then the estate people. Honestly Lexi, the guy was an arrogant prick and I didn't like him. I just wanted to be sure everything was good with you."

"Yeah, everything is fine. I mean no one has contacted me about anything."

"Good. That's what I want to hear. And if anyone does, don't hesitate to call me Lexi."

"Thanks, I will."

"Ok you take care Lexi and don't forget, the LAPD loves your truffles."

"I'll be sure to send some as soon as I am up and running. Thanks Detective Moore."

I hang up the phone and I'm pissed. I lost my best friend and now people I don't even know think I stole her stuff. Arrogant prick is being kind. Who the hell is this guy? And why would he think I did anything wrong? I can feel the ball of grief that sits at the pit of stomach turning into a fireball of rage. It is remarkable how closely intertwined sadness and anger can be. I need to not let my mind spiral down that path. This is something I have no control over. I did nothing wrong. I keep reminding myself of that. But if I didn't do anything wrong, why is my grief constantly blanketed with guilt?

I need to shift gears. I need light and sun. I need to think happy thoughts. I have to focus on what is going on right now. I can't dwell on what has already happened. I have a business I am starting. I have a date with a handsome man tonight. And if Ashley were here, she'd tell me to get over myself and start enjoying life. I smile. She would be right. The universe has made that perfectly clear to me one too many times. Life is short, extremely short.

So, here I am, laying by the Charles, music playing on my IPhone; I am trying to relax and refocus my angry thoughts to more positive ones. My phone is on vibrate and off it goes, I try to ignore it because I begin to daydream about the events in front of me. I quickly stop myself. Expectations are a very bad thing in my book, almost as bad as dwelling in the past. I think one can be excited about something and look forward to it, but setting expectations, that are truly only made up in your head, and no one else knows about them, can be very dangerous. Seriously, we've all done it and we will continue to do it no matter how many times it bites us in the ass.

We do it on many levels. Sometimes, it's very innocent, we expect the party to be fun, or perhaps a big sale we expected to come in fell through and because of this we expect things at our company to be tense. But I am talking about the expectations or full on stories we make up in our heads. The fatal flaw of the single woman, the relationship created in our heads, (perhaps men do it to, but I can really only speak about my own gender). It is basically like speed dating only with yourself. You meet some guy and set up a first date. The time leading up to the date you typically tell someone about the dude and the date you are going on. That someone usually asks a lot of questions about this person, none of which you know the answer to, because, well, you haven't gone on a date yet. But this starts the spin cycle of expectations in your head. You begin to wonder what the night will be like; will he be funny? What might he ask me? How will I respond? What should I ask him? I wonder if he will kiss me?

Oh, the kiss, we can spend hours thinking about the first kiss. It is so telling as we all know, I mean because really if the guy can't kiss, forget about it. Then of course, because it is in our head, he's a great kisser, we go out again, next thing you know, we're thinking about meeting parents, perhaps a weekend somewhere, and what life will be like on Sundays when we wake up together. It is friggin' crazy where our heads will go. The problem of course, it is all in OUR heads. So, to avoid an incredibly disappointing situation on a first date because he didn't stick to the script that I wrote in my head, I try to not think about the date ahead of time. This rule is especially adhered to, if I am looking forward to said date. Now, again, no one is perfect, random hot guy, in my head, unbelievable kisser!

I eventually leave my spot on the dock and stroll back to my apartment. I managed to ignore six phone calls and an unknown number of emails. It was time to face the music. Once I arrive home, I throw on some tunes and a pot of coffee. I glance at the clock, it is three in the afternoon, shit, I still have about three hours of work to do and Nick is picking me up at eight. Normally I would leave myself forty-five minutes to get ready, however, admittedly I'm a bit nervous for tonight so I know me, I am going to need at least two hours. I need forty-five minutes to shower and do my hair. I then have to leave an hour and fifteen minutes to go through the six different outfits, twice, that I may wear, of course, as always, going back to the original outfit I put on. Why do we do that?

I head over to my desk and start going through my lists and listening to voicemails. Things have become a bit more complicated now as I try and shift away from one business and open up another. I find myself working a lot. But I know this routine, when you own your own company there is no such thing as a weekend. Then again, there is no such thing as a meeting with your boss either.

It is ten minutes before eight at night, I have managed to get through a mountain of paperwork, take a shower, get myself dressed and shove all of the outfits I rejected back into my closet. Ten minutes before Nick gets here and I am completely nervous. I try to breath, drink water, and think about happy, calm thoughts, but none of it seems to be working. My palms are sweaty and I feel a bit jumpy. "Calm down Lexi!" I repeat to myself over and over again. I don't know why I am so nervous; I have been on a ton of first dates. And I have been on quite a few with people I was really interested in, so this is not new to me.

I pace between my bedroom and living room occasionally stopping to peer out my bedroom window onto Beacon Street to see if I can spot Nick. I don't. Something does however catch my eye. I take a closer look and can't believe my eyes. There is Patrick walking hand and hand with a woman right by my building. "Huh, well he just got more interesting." I think to myself. Just as I was staring a little more closely, like a nosey neighbor peering out the window, Patrick looks up. I jumped away from my window. My curiosity is running wild. Obviously it's beyond fine if Patrick is dating other women. We only had one date and I am going out with another man. But why would Patrick walk by my building with another woman? That is a mistake I wouldn't have made. He's a rookie. My phone rings and it is Nick. My curiosity about Patrick is back to zero.

"Hey there." I answer.

"Well hello Lexi, your chariot awaits."

"Great, I'll be right down." I hang up the phone and do one last quick check in the mirror. I'm not really sure why, at this point, there isn't anything I can do.

I bounce out of my building and there is Nick, standing on the sidewalk. I look behind him and I see his black BMW SUV double parked with the hazard lights on. *Very nice touch*, I think to myself, *he actually stepped out of his car to wait for me.*

Nick greeted me with a big smile on his face, kissed my cheek, took a step back and said, "You look amazing."

"Thank you. It's nice to see you."

Nick opens my door for me, waits until I got in and shut it. Again, I am such a sucker for a chivalrous man.

Nick ended up choosing one of my favorite restaurants in the South End, Mistral. Great food, great atmosphere, and valet parking! We decided to forgo the table he had reserved for a spot in their beautiful bar area. I am typically a "belly-up" kind of girl. I love great food and wine; I just like to enjoy it in a more laid back style. I welcome taking a comfortable seat at a bar over sitting at a table. Besides, if you really like someone, it's nice not to have a table stuck between the two of you.

The evening was spectacular. As far as first dates are concerned I would give this one an A+. Nick is kind, and relaxed. He scored major points for choosing some great wine. The conversation flowed, we laughed, did a few of the leg touches along the way, engaged in conversation with other people at the bar. It was just plain fun. Well and of course the fact that I find the man dead sexy is a plus!

When we finished our dinner, Nick and I jumped into his car and decided that we were having too much fun and 10:30 was too early to end a Saturday night. We found a parking spot on the block in front of my building and strolled over to Commonwealth Avenue to grab a nightcap at yet another one of my favorite spots, The Eastern Standard. And since the Red Sox were out of town, the crowd was just the perfect size, and you could grab a seat; yet, not feel as though you had the place to yourselves. We continued our perfect evening, chatting away, occasionally engaging others.

We finished our wine and headed out the door. It was a beautiful night and Commonwealth Avenue is a beautiful Boston street. We crossed over the northbound side of Commonwealth Avenue to one of the grassy park like settings that splits the north and southbound sides of Commonwealth Avenue. Once there, Nick stopped and turned towards me, "I had a great time Lexi. I mean really great."

I smile, "As did I Nick. You are a lot of fun."

"I would really like to see you again Lexi."

"Well, then you should." I reply, trying to lighten up his serious tone.

Nick laughs and pulls me towards him and gives me a huge hug. Nick gently pushed me ever so slightly away from him and kisses the top of my forehead. I smile and look up at him our faces only inches apart. His features are striking even in the dimly lit park, his thick dark wavy hair, perfect green eyes, soft skin, and thick lips. He held my gaze and gently grabs my face with both of his strong hands. He kisses me gently on the lips. He pulls back for a second still holding my face in his hands, smiles ever so slightly and kisses me again. This time, his mouth slightly open and I could just feel a brush of his tongue. Our lips part, his hands still holding my face, he just stares for a second and smiles. Nick grabs my hand and we start walking.

We make it back to my building, both smiling wide. Nick lets out a big sigh and kisses me gently on the lips, wraps his arms around my waist lifting me off the ground a bit and whispering, "I know what I'm going to be dreaming about tonight."

"Baseball." I reply.

"You're awesome." Nick laughs, "Get inside and sleep well. I will call you. Are you allowed to go out on a school night?"

"Sometimes" I reply, "And thank you Nick, I had a great time."

I turn and head into my building; I look back and Nick is standing there, making sure I am in behind the locked doors; he blows me a kiss and heads to his car. I float up to my apartment, grinning from ear to ear. Chemistry does funny things to people and this man makes my insides jump.

6

SUNDAY DINNER WITH TY

I wake up Sunday morning still smiling from the night before. What a frigging awesome date. I happily jump out of bed and put on a pot of coffee, thinking about Nick, his kiss, everything. I look out my window to the Charles and the water is like glass, the calm before the storm. The sky is gray and the storm clouds are dark as I look down the river. I flip on my computer and check the weather, nothing but rain and thunderstorms all day. A perfect Sunday in my book! I missed these days when I lived in Los Angeles. It rarely rained there and I would find myself craving the rain so I would have an excuse to stay inside, not shower, watch movies, and eat junk food all day. With all of the craziness that has gone one over the last week, my lease signing, my fun date with Patrick, my amazing date with Nick, my creepy stranger, and the call from Detective Moore; I needed a little down time. And, of course, it is Sunday, my fun night with Ty.

I say night, but typically, Ty and I get together by four in the afternoon, it is technically a school night after all, so we need to start early. And then my phone, with the beep, beep, like clockwork, every Sunday Ty sends me a text at seven-thirty in the morning.

I grab my phone and read Ty's Text: *Good morning sunshine. Can't wait to see you later and hear all about this new man, 4 pm, my place or yours, are we cooking our ordering out?*

I text back: *Let's cook, my place, I'll figure out the menu and shop, how about red?*

Done, see you at 4, was his response.

I love the friendship Ty and I have. We don't have issues, we don't have to say, "what can I bring?" or feel badly about saying, "Hey, pick this up on the way." We have been doing this for over two years now and it just runs smoothly. Again, God forbid, either one of us actually commits to someone and we need to give up our Sundays. It certainly doesn't hurt any woman to have a best, extremely handsome, single guy friend to discuss with all of your issues. He calms me down when I need it, he is my voice of reason, and he is the shoulder I've cried on.

Crying is something I do often. For me it's not about whether or not I cry, because I will cry, it is more about how out of control was the crying. Ty experienced one that was monumental. Most people have not seen that side of me. I am a suffer- in-solitude kind of girl. If I am feeling sad I tend to isolate, hence, most people I know, know I have been sad, or have become sad, but have never really seen me full on in tears curled up on the floor, the couch, or leaning against the kitchen cabinets. Yes, these are all places I have found myself crying. It's not like I say to myself, I think I'll go curl up on the bathroom floor and cry for a while, it is just where I end up when the flood of tears come. I don't cry to that level all that often, but when I do, boy, those tears just come and are hard to stop. I break easily, and I feel pain, but I also heal quickly. And, if I feel emotion, I sit with it. If I have to cry I cry, if I am angry I am angry, I do not deny myself the feelings, I just try to temper my reactions. As with most things in my life, sometimes I am better at tempering than others. I have certainly shot off my fair share of post break up angry emails and text messages.

So there I was, about two years ago. I had just moved back to Boston and started to date this guy who I really liked. I got ahead of myself. He was a very handsome, smart, successful man who seemed solid in his own life. He stood about 6" 2, big brown eyes and a fabulous smile. He had a strong physical presence but his words and his touch were soft and kind. I fell for him, it happens. Unfortunately, he really wasn't as available as I had hoped. He was very focused on his career and was always travelling. I mean this man must have traveled just about every day of the year. Now, I was travelling quite often as well, but I was starting to burn out so my focus was on other parts of my life. Here in lies a great problem. His career was really starting to take off, mine was in need of a change, so my attention went more to him; and his attention, exactly where it should have been, his career. And, what big mistake did I make? I let my head get ahead of the relationship and fell into the fabulous trap of creating things in my head that I thought could be but were not. I saw some potential and ran with it; thus, leading to major disappointment on my part, to some fault of his but mostly created by my own doing. Then I would be angry and hurt, and well, you know how the cycle works. I was falling in love with what could be, not with what was. That's a recipe for major heartache and that's exactly what happened.

One random Sunday morning in June, I had been back in Boston about six months and dating this man for three, everything came to a head. We ended it. I jumped on a plane that afternoon and went to nurture clients, a great distraction from my own heartache. As I have mentioned, I had become very good at compartmentalizing and that is exactly what I did. However, I can only do that for so long and when I do, my breakdown is a bit more severe than it may have been if I just let myself feel the emotion in the moment; but sometimes you just can't.

Anyway, I came home from my trip on a Thursday night. It was a rainy June night. I was tired. I landed at Logan, waited at the baggage claim, grabbed my bag and headed to the taxi cab stand, jumped into the cab and headed on the short fifteen minute ride home; a routine with which I was all too familiar. I remember feeling exceptionally exhausted that night, more than likely due to the fact that I had been harboring feelings that I couldn't release, all the while dealing with my clients' emotional pain. I remember thinking that I was really sick of going it alone. I wanted a partner, I wanted to go home and not necessarily vent to someone, I just wanted to curl up with someone. I was sick of going to bed alone every night. I was done with being alone. I remember feeling the tears begin to well up in my eyes. I tried to think about other things I needed to do, in order to spare the cab driver from listening to me cry in his backseat. I barely managed to get through the ride.

I walked into my building, suitcase in tow, and fortunately, no one was in the lobby or in the elevator as I stepped in. I wasn't in the mood to "fake" happy. I watched as the elevator lit up each floor number as it passed. It could not get to the ninth floor fast enough. *Almost there*, I was thinking. I knew once I got into my apartment and shut the door, I would release everything. It's almost like when you have to really go to the bathroom and you're almost there, it seems as though your need to go gets exponentially worse the closer you get to the bathroom. That is how I was feeling at that moment; I was barely holding back the tears. I ran down the hall when I got off the elevator, keys in hand I unlocked my apartment door, let go of my suitcase handle, my door slammed behind me and I just stood there as tears started to stream down my face. It was so overwhelming I wasn't even making any noise. I didn't move, I covered my mouth with both hands, stood still and silently cried.

I wasn't crying over the lost relationship, that was just the last straw. I was crying over the many lost relationships, the loneliness, the overwhelming emotional toll my career was starting to take and the loss of control I was starting to feel. I was crying for all the losses in my life. I was crying about the secret I was keeping. The trauma and devastation that happen in California, that no one knew about because I still wasn't able to speak about it. I was crying because my parents died when I was five, because my grandparents had passed and because I did not have one living relative that I knew of. Even though I was living in the middle of a major city and I could hear the people and the noise from the city streets, even though my life was rich with friends and purpose, I was crying because I was feeling so very alone. I was tired. I was tired of walking through my apartment door alone, taking cabs alone, walking into restaurants alone, flying alone. Although surrounded by people, I was alone. I did not want to keep walking through this life by myself.

I eventually took a few steps and moved off the hardwood floor and onto my shag rug, where I just collapsed into a ball on my carpet and sobbed. And that is exactly where Ty found me.

I always texted Ty whenever I landed. It was a funny thing he liked me to do. I texted him when I got to Logan ending it with a sad face, he texted back but I never responded, which made him worry. Ty came over to my building and security knew him well and I had told them they could always let Ty in, so they did. I had entered my apartment so fast that I forgot to lock the door. I can only imagine what was going through Ty's head at the time. He knocked on my door and then opened it. He entered to find my bag laying there in the entry way and me curled up on my living room rug, still in my long black trench coat, sobbing.

Ty had called out my name as he opened my apartment door so somewhere through the sobbing I realized it was him and knew I didn't have to move; I could just keep doing what I was doing. Ty came racing over to me, knelt down next to me and in a panicked voice asked if I was okay as he brushed the hair out of my face. I still had my hands covering my mouth and I nodded.

"Lexi, are you hurt?" he asked.

I shook my head no and he let out a sigh of relief. After a few seconds, I felt his hands slip underneath me; he picked me up off the floor, carried me to my bed, and gently laid me down. He left the room for a moment returning with tissues and water. He then lay down beside me, rubbed my back, kissed my head and stayed there, all night.

A dear friend of mine describes these moments as "Universe Winks." She describes them as the moments in your life when you think you cannot possibly take one more step, you feel as though you have been beaten up, lost your way, or maybe karma is just kicking your ass. Then at that moment, when you need it most, the universe steps in and winks at you. You may not get all the pain taken away, or everything that you are asking for, but you get just what you need to give you the strength to keep walking.

As the sun started to stream into my bedroom the next morning, I woke up. My head was pounding from all of the crying I had done. I could sense that my eyes were puffy. At some point in the night I had taken off my trench coat and shoes, as they were lying on the floor next to my bed, but I still had on the clothes from the day before. My back was to Ty, his arms were wrapped around my waist, and as I started to stir, he just pulled me a little closer. And we lay there for a little longer; the two friends that we were, on top of my covers, fully clothed, but not alone, and that was my wink.

The coffee maker beeping telling me the coffee is ready snaps me back to reality. I pour myself a mug of coffee and realize that my eyes are watering. Thinking back to that moment in time, I can still feel the pain and my complete gratefulness to Ty. Then a smile comes to my face thinking about the wonderful relaxing afternoon/night we will share. I don't know what I would do without him.

All of this of course may have you asking why I am not dating Ty. I don't know. I am acutely aware that I am great with friendships and bad with relationships. I'm afraid of losing Ty. I don't think I could handle losing one more person I love. And, well, if I don't date him then I can assure the fact that I won't screw anything up and he will remain in my life. Besides, Ty did not start dating anyone until recently. And from how he describes the women he dates they are the complete opposite of me. He likes tall brunettes who look like they just walked out of a beauty salon, all of the time. You know, their hair is perfect, make-up and nails are perfect, and their outfits are flawless. I'm attractive but more in the "girl next door", way. Besides it takes me two hours to put together an outfit. I can't grow three inches, I think I would look horrible as a brunette, and heck my nails chip thirty minutes after getting them done. I am not his relationship type, but I'm his friend type. Well, I may not get to sleep with the most handsome man on earth, but I do get to be his friend, his best friend. I still win. I have also convinced myself through my imagination that he is a horrendous kisser and a bull in a china shop in bed. It helps.

I down my cup of coffee and jump into the shower. I do, have some shopping to do. I throw on my favorite Sunday outfit, jeans, flip-flops and a tee shirt and make my shopping list. I hate that I have to make a shopping list, but I do. I can keep names, numbers, appointments, and critical facts in my head, but god forbid I go to the grocery store without a list. If I go to get ten things I come back with thirty, of which only five were a part of the original ten that I needed. I am 38 and losing it! I pour another mug of coffee before I take off, I check my phone and see six new text messages.

Six, I think to myself, all while I was in the shower and it's not even eight-thirty on a Sunday morning, damn, that's like a text jackpot.

I take a look at my texts, one from Lindsay, one from Renee, and one from Zoe, all inquiring about my date with Nick, shocking. I then see one from Nick, now that was a bit of a surprise. It reads:

> *Good Morning Lexi, I know, breaking the three-day rule before I text. Whatever, I had a great time and can't wait to see you Tuesday.*

"Tuesday," I think to myself. "What is Tuesday?"

I rack my brain trying to remember what I agreed to do on Tuesday. I had a few glasses of wine and was certainly child-like happy on my date with Nick, but by no means tipsy. I could not for the life of me remember agreeing to anything on Tuesday. Suddenly I get it. He is a clever fellow. So I respond:

> *Hi Nick, I too had a great time and am so looking forward to Tuesday. I have been dying to see the Vagina Monologues! Shall I meet you at the Opera House?*

Let's see how he handles that one. I look at the next text and lo and behold it is from Patrick and read:

> *Good morning Lexi, I just got in late last night, but was wondering if you were free tonight, perhaps I could coax you into dinner?*

Hmmm, I ponder my response. He just got in? From where? His date? I decide to be nice and respond:

> *Hi Patrick, welcome home! I am having dinner with my friend Ty tonight, but perhaps another day?*

I looked at the sixth text and to my surprise it was from the man whom I dated when I first moved back to Boston. Yes, the guy who precipitated the major melt down. Again, not the cause just the last straw. It read:

> *Hi Lexi! It's Dom, how are you? I know it has been awhile but would love to see you and catch up.*

Wow, I don't even have time to deal with that one right now.

I head to my couch with my coffee in hand, sit down and try and take in the fact that he just texted me after all of this time! Please! And then another text, from Nick

> *No way, I will pick you up at 6:30 p.m.; the show starts at 7:00 p.m. We can grab some food after. Can't wait.*

Damn, the man is good. I reply:

> *Looking forward to it* ☺

That kind of backfired on me. I was just joking. I don't want to see the Vagina Monologues with a dude I have been on one date with. I don't want to see it with any guy. I need to think about this and fix it before he actually buys the tickets. Shit.

For the next two hours I proceed to schedule a date with Patrick for Wednesday night, I had to, I am just so curious about this guy. I speak with all of my girls and give them the goods on Nick, that I am going out with Patrick on Wednesday, as well as my surprise text from Dominic.

After I finally hang up the phone I feel as though I could go back to bed. Shit, what am I doing? I am closing operations on my consulting business, opening a new business in two months and now starting to date. Wow, this is going to be a busy fall, careful what you wish for.

And then there is Dominic, the infamous Dominic. I guess since I am being honest here I should tell you a bit more about Dominic. I'll be brief. We had another encounter after that dreadful day in June. Ok, we had a few more encounters. No bullshit, we had two more additional three month long flings. I know, crazy. Truth is, I was going through a difficult time, and there was something about Dominic. I still to this day cannot put my finger on what it is about him that drove me so crazy. He was, well is, handsome and very smart. But in reality, the sex was just ok and he was never available. And there it is. He was never available. A very smart, handsome man, who, I really probably wouldn't want to spend any major time with; however, he was unavailable. He was just what I needed when I returned to Boston from Los Angeles. He was my excuse, my drama, and my chaos. He kept my questioning friends at bay. He kept my own questioning at bay. At the time it worked. At the time, or I should say times, I was unaware of all of the above. I actually convinced myself I was totally into this rarely seen, once in a while guy, and that it was working for me. So, not once, not twice, but three times I felt the heartache.

There were however, nights filled with tears. The nights curled up in my bed crying my eyes out. During those nights, in the wee hours of the morning, when I would lie awake trying to shake off my angst; I realized one of two things is definitely going to happen, either I will fall asleep or the sun will rise. Unfortunately for me, they usually happened at the same time. But they happened. And I moved on, hopefully learning a thing or two.

So now as I look at Dominic's text, I think about how incredibly arrogant he is. But of course, he is, it has worked three other times, why wouldn't it work now? And I am reminded of a great cliché, "Fool me once, shame on you, fool me twice, shame on me." I guess I would add fool me four times and I am the biggest idiot on the planet. And so I, unceremoniously, deleted his text. It felt great!

Ty shows up to my apartment promptly at four in the afternoon. He waltz's in saying, "Where is my sexy baby girl?"

I love his pet names for me; it always puts a big smile on my face. He walks into my open kitchen living room space, shakes off the water as it is now raining buckets outside, places two bottles of rather good red wine on the counter and comes over and gives me a kiss on the cheek and a big squeeze.

"Mmm," he starts, "something smells good!"

"I think it is coming from next door, all I've done is roast almonds." I smirk. "Two bottles, Ty? And nice ones I will say, what's the occasion?"

"Well, one is for today, and the other is a little congratulations on yet another step forward to making me a very fat man!"

I laugh, "I just signed the lease Ty, it hasn't opened yet."

"I know, but that is the biggest commitment I have ever seen you make. So, it's a congratulations on a medium step towards establishing roots and settling down."

"Ty, in my world we call it settling in, not down, never down."

Ty and I begin to go to work on our feast, chopping and sautéing, all while discussing our weekend events. Ty's world has been constantly focused on work, as the real estate markets are still volatile. At times I can really see the stress on his face. I think it comes less from concern about him and more about the agents who work for him. Of course, not surprising, that is Ty, the take care of everyone else guy.

Ty and I cook and talk and joke for two and a half hours, then finally belly up to my kitchen bar to dine and sip wine.

"Okay Ty, so I get that you had yet another boring date last night. But what is with that, are you hiding something? I'm finding it hard to believe that EVERY date you go on is boring."

"What are you talking about?" Ty inquires with a disgusted look on his face, "Not every date I am on is boring Lexi, I never call our dates boring."

"Very funny and nice try Ty, spill."

"Lexi, I am being perfectly honest. There is nothing to it really. I mean, I just have had a bad streak with boring women. And, certainly, lately I have not had much time considering all of the stress with my business."

"I know, I'm worried about you Ty, sometimes the stress is so evident on your face. How are you holding up?"

"I am, and it will be fine, there is no need to worry about me. And as far as the women, in a lot of ways Lexi, I am like you. I am picky; I need to feel that spark. I passed your infamous 'two year' mark, so who knows, maybe soon I will be with her."

I think for a second and then begin, "You know Ty, there is more to the 'two-year rule', it is not just about time."

"I know," Ty begins, "and I think I've done a good job getting out there and keeping appropriate boundaries, knowing where I am and hopefully not breaking too many hearts."

"Ty, look at you, trust me, hearts have been broken, though no fault of yours. What I mean is, there is a moment during those years, however many there are, there is a shift that happens."

Ty looks at me puzzled, so I continue, "It's as if, with someone getting sober for the first time, they work so hard at trying to get sober and work the program, go to meetings, and do all of the right things. They are determined to be the perfect sober person. They are so focused on the actions they need to do that they miss the whole concept of how to live a life of recovery. The same behaviors, and anxieties and feelings that led them to substances are now working against them as they try to maintain their sobriety. Then all of the sudden they have this moment, where they realize 'I am right where I am supposed to be' they realize sobriety is not a chapter in a book or a task to be finished or checked off. They come to understand that sobriety is life. They begin to understand that there is a force bigger than them, and fighting it is impossible. They all of the sudden, feel peace, because, just accepting today, the moment, the right now, is a hell of a lot easier than all of the energy they were putting into to trying to be the best sober person. And again Ty, I am completely butchering this concept, but I had a shift."

Ty holds up his hand with a perplexed look on his face, "Wait, what, you had one? Were you in recovery?"

"No," I respond. "Well, maybe, recovery from my addiction to relationships and the search of the love that everyone tells me is out there. In a way I guess it is very similar. Someone who uses is often in search of the original fantastic high they felt, but have lost as the addiction gets stronger, or to cover the immense pain they feel on a daily basis. Sometimes they do it to feel normal or feel like how they think everyone else is feeling. Yes, in that way, that is exactly what I would do. I was constantly seeking to experience that 'high' you get when you first fall for someone, and to find what everyone else seemed to have. And all I got was perhaps, a fleeting moment of the rush of endorphins through my body and then a flood of sleepless nights, tears, heartache, or guilt if I hurt someone. And I suffered all of the aftermath of my poor decisions. I was so focused on the idea that if I do X, Y, and Z, I will make love happen in my life. I was so focused on next steps that I wasn't ever present in the moment."

Ty takes a breath and shakes his head as he tries to absorb all of the information, and then asks, "So what happened, when was your shift?"

"Honestly Ty, it was about six months after you came to my rescue, while I laid sobbing on that rug." I point to the shag rug next to us and raise my eyebrows as I glance his way.

Ty's wonderful brown eyes soften as he looks at me with a half-smile, half pouting lip.

"Remember how crazy I was with dating and men after that?"

"Yeah," Ty responds quietly.

"I went to town Ty, dating everyone in sight. I had poor boundaries, I made poor decisions, I would cry over someone I barely knew. I felt like I had to be in a serious relationship, I needed that. I needed what everyone else around me apparently had. I wasn't ready and the universe was making that loud and clear. It was telling me, 'keep doing what you're doing Lexi, and all you're going to get is pain.' I wasn't happy in my life so I was trying to fill a void. And I wanted it filled quickly."

"And?" Ty asks.

"Well, it was uneventful actually. It was about mid-January and I was outside smoking a butt and all of the sudden it just hit me. It was after I had really over reacted to some guy blowing me off and I was feeling crappy and angry with myself for even giving this guy the time of day and then to have so much emotion about it. I was thinking, Lexi, you don't even know this guy, you two have nothing in common; why are you being so crazy? And then this peace just came over me. I started to review all of the poor decisions. The things I would do for people I didn't even know. I would buy a whole new outfit, blow off tons of work, spend hours in preparation for a date, with someone, I barely knew. This dictated my life. I would continually repeat that pattern and then be angry when it didn't work out. Yeah, I was angry, but not at them."

I continued, "I was in search of the high Ty and trying to fill a void, and in doing so, made bad choices. I just realized I needed to fill the void myself, I didn't need to be in a rush, life is going to happen, stop trying to control it, I finally got the Serenity Prayer on a whole new level, and I calmed down."

"How does that go again?" Ty asks.

"God grant me the serenity to accept the things I cannot change, courage to change the things I can, and wisdom to know the difference."

"And do you feel better?" Ty asks.

"Hell yes!" I reply, "Ty, look at me, look at all of the changes I have made and the forward progress in my own life. And really, how many calls have you received from me in the last year and half ranting and raving over some dude?"

"Shit, Lexi, none."

"Exactly."

"Yeah but now you have two guys going, are you making up for lost time?" Ty inquires, rather seriously.

"I don't have two men 'going'. I went on two first dates with two different men. One I kissed, one I did not. And now I happen to be going on two second dates with the same two different men. No harm done, nothing physical. A girl's gotta eat Ty."

Ty laughs, "Ah, yes, little do they know the trouble that awaits them."

"What?" I gasp, "I'm not trouble, just having fun, what's wrong with dating?"

"Seriously, Lexi, do you like one more than the other?"

"One date with each Ty, I'm really trying not to get into my old patterns of jumping ahead. I don't know either of these men. Dating is about having fun in the moment. And that is all it is, a moment."

"I don't think I've had a shift Lexi." Ty says bringing the conversation back to its serious tone.

"Ty, not everyone does. The addiction to love was my issue; I needed two years plus a moment. You may have something else to discover, or not, maybe you just haven't met the right girl."

Ty stared through me and gave me the infamous man "hmmm."

"Ty, do you want to expand upon that hmmm?"

Ty laughs, "Uh-oh, I just gave you the 'man hmmm,' your favorite. Actually, Lexi, contrary to your belief, that there is always more to the 'man hmmm' than what is being said, I really don't have anything more to add. I mean I probably do, I just feel as though I need to think about it first."

"Ty, overthinking can get you into trouble as well. You are the most sane, wonderful man I have ever met. Honestly, maybe you just haven't met her and that is all there is to it."

"I think I have met her Lexi, I just… I'm not quite ready."

"What?" I exclaim. "You have met her? Who? When? Who?"

Ty laughs. "It is complicated Lexi."

"Do you work with her?"

Ty just gives me his soft brown eyes and a slight smile. "Sort of. Trust me, when I'm ready to pursue anything I will discuss it with you first."

"You're killing me Ty."

"I know." He says, as his smile gets bigger.

7

MONDAY THERAPY

My weekend was mixed to say the least. I was all over the place from sleepless and anxiety riddled on Friday night to on cloud nine after one date Saturday night. And I can't seem to stop thinking about this woman that Ty seems to really like. When did this happen? And to top it all off, having the conversation with Detective Moore ultimately has caused more angst than I would like. I really need to get serious about dealing with my emotions around everything that happened to Ashley. I emailed my friend Jackie, who also happens to be my on and off again therapist.

Jackie and I went to graduate school together. Some people judge me for this, seeing a friend who is a therapist. Of course some people just like to tell you things you are doing wrong. I typically ignore those people. Seeing a therapist, who is a friend of mine, doesn't even make my list of top 100 things I have done wrong in my life.

"Hey Lex." Jackie says as she stands up, walks out from her desk and gives me a hug.

"Hey Jackie, thanks so much for squeezing me in on such short notice."

I take a seat on Jackie's couch and she plops herself in her leather chair across from me. Jackie is brilliant. I know this. She, like everyone else has her own baggage to work through. However, when we are in her office, in these seats, she is completely focused on helping me. The other great thing about us both being therapists and friends; we don't waste any time while we are in her office. We save niceties and catching up on general life stuff for coffee or phone calls. When we are here, we are here to work. And we both know I have a lot of work to do.

"Lexi, I have been thinking a lot about our last session." Jackie jumps right in.

"Our last session? Jackie that was three months ago."

"I know." Jackie says as she rolls her eyes at me. "How are you sleeping?"

"Intermittently."

"And your anxiety?"

"It's high. I'm obviously at a very stressful time with work, closing one business and opening another one."

"Have you had any more of those unsettling instances like the one you told me about a few weeks back?" Jackie inquires.

"You mean with the strange person I saw?"

"Yes."

"No." Then I thought for a second. "No wait, I did. I saw him again. On the Mass Ave bridge. Ugh, God Jackie. I don't know what to think, he could just be a creepy guy who lives in my neighborhood. I'm paranoid."

"Well I was hoping you would be willing to try something and hear me out before you say no."

I smile at Jackie. "Okay."

"I would like you to tell me about Ashley."

Just hearing Ashley's name brought an overwhelming sense of despair over me. I could feel a lump in my throat and my eyes begin to fill with tears.

Jackie quickly continues as she watches my composure begin to fall apart. "I'm not asking you to talk about the incident, or her death. I want you to tell me the story of her, from the beginning. From when you first met."

It is a good idea. I want to talk about Ashley. That is why I am here. I understand intellectually what Jackie is trying to get me to do.

But I am overwhelmed. Just thinking of Ashley, and hearing Jackie say 'her death' leaves me distraught. I try to contain them at first, the tears. But I fail. It's a piercing pain. It starts in my gut, and then travels up to my heart, wraps itself around my heart and squeezes it. Then the lump in my throat that forms, I know if I say one thing, if I think one more thing, I will not be able to stop the rush of tears. I hang my head and sob.

After about ten minutes, I think I am done. I begin to calm down and then something happens. I'm not sure what, a thought, a vision, something and I start sobbing all over again. Another ten minutes go by.

"Lexi," Jackie says as she hands me another tissue.

"You know Jackie," I stop speaking to blow my nose. I can feel the puffiness of my face and I can barely breathe as my nose is all stuffed. I do some breathing, deep breaths in and long slow exhales out.

I clear my throat and try again. "Every time I find myself busting into tears on a random Tuesday, crying myself to sleep, or curled up on the bathroom floor sobbing, I think to myself, 'okay, that was a good one, I think you really got it all out this time. I think that will be the last time you cry over this.' Whether I am crying over a man, a broken heart, or Ashley, I always find myself asking *why*. And no matter what the question, big or small: Why did she die? Why couldn't I help her? Why did I drink that much? Why did he leave? Why is the question that drives all of us crazy; yet, the most difficult to let go of. Once you do, you know that is when you can move forward. But sometimes you will never know and you have to be willing to let go of why, and walk away. Or sprint, if you can."

"Funny actually, most would say of me that I am very good at running away. And I have tried to run away from the pain. I try and forget that I don't know the answer to why. The pain, it keeps coming, not matter what I do, there it is. It's at the end of every cigarette, the bottom of every wine glass, or Ben and Jerry's container. It is at the end of every long run, long flight, or long day. It's always right there, no matter how hard I try to avoid it. So, I have learned, I just have to feel it and eventually, it begins to dissipate. But this time, it's not dissipating Jackie."

"What questions are you constantly asking yourself Lexi?"

"Why didn't I do more? Why didn't I stop it? Why," I pause, that is as far as I can go.

"Yes, those questions would keep anyone up at night. I don't know the story Lexi. But I know you are here. You are living. My question is how do you want to live?"

"Happily ever after."

"How can you do that?"

"I don't know."

"What do you need to let go of Lexi?"

"My anger, my fear, my guilt."

"One at a time. Why are you angry?"

"I'm angry because that scum bag killed her. He took away my best friend. And why? For what reason? She was amazing. Who does that? And now I am loaded with guilt because I didn't do enough, I didn't stop it."

"How could you have stopped it Lexi?"

"I don't know. But I run through it in my mind all of the time. If only I was there."

"Lexi, you couldn't have stopped it. You can't control other people. And you are not responsible for their actions. He did this, not you."

"I know Jackie. Intellectually, I know this. You know what else I know, the people I love die and I survive."

"You mean because of the car accident?"

"Yes, I was in that car too. I survived and my parents died."

"I understand that Lexi. But how does that translate to Ashley? You weren't there."

"Because I..." I shake my head. I can't say it. I'm not ready.

"It's okay, Lexi. We will get there. How about you keep coming to see me every Monday?"

"Okay."

"I mean every Monday Lexi. We need to get through the story, together, everything that happened. I am here to do this with you Lexi."

I nod and glance at the clock. "Yes. But for now, I am going to have to stuff this all back in my little box and get a move on. See you next week, I promise."

"Lexi, I'm serious. I am worried about you."

"I know. I want to get through this. I have to. I can't keep falling apart every time I hear her name."

"Good, see you next week then."

I leave Jackie's office and quickly put on my sunglasses to hide the evidence of my sobbing. Jackie's office is in Beacon Hill about a twenty-minute walk from my house. Which means I have approximately that much time to pull myself together and re-focus my energy and emotions from past events to my future business.

When I met Ashley in Los Angeles, it changed everything. With all of its glitz, glamour, and pretty people it was easy to feel insignificant, lost, and lonely in the City of Angels. My friendship with Ashley changed all of that. I began to see LA through her rose-colored glasses. Ashley was the kind of woman who saw the best in everything and brought out the best in everyone. Well, almost everyone. Our friendship was the greatest thing I got from LA. Her murder was the worst.

It has been a few years since her murder. A day doesn't go by when I don't think of her. But months can go by without me thinking of her murder. I can separate the two. I can think of her and miss her and not think of the act that took her away. However, then, sometimes, something, like the call from Detective Moore, will remind me of the murder. And that is when the negative energy and emotions begin to overwhelm my world.

I miss her. If she were here, she would be so excited about my new business. She would be flooding me with emails, phone calls, and text messages filled with great ideas for my shop. She would be planning her trip out here to help me launch my dream. I inhaled quickly to try and suck back my tears. Ashley wouldn't want anything to stand in my way if she were here. *The people I love die and I survive.* Guilt is an extraordinarily heavy emotion.

8

THE FIRST SECOND DATE

Monday did eventually turn around for me. I spent the afternoon working with my graphic designer. We chose a great logo, wrote all of the copy for the website and brochure, and created invitation designs for the pre-opening parties. I slept a bit better last night; however, I did wake up a few times feeling anxious. I think that is something I am going to have to tolerate for a while. Ashley would want my business to succeed. She is not here but I am. She was better at living than I am. I need to honor her by trying to live like she did. I have decided that no matter what happens the day before, I am, from this point forward, going to start each day with a conscious positive outlook. I have invested a lot of time and money into starting this new business and it has to work.

I have a day of tedious tasks ahead of me. I am creating my contact lists for all of the concierges, event, and wedding planners. Basically a list of key people who could potentially refer me significant business. Focusing on my date tonight with Nick helps me face the notion that I will be spending most of my day in front of the computer.

By noon my eyes feel like they are on fire and my muscles stiff from sitting. I grab my city satchel and keys and head out, as it is time to get some fresh air, movement, and food. I pop out onto Beacon Street and am greeted by a stiffly wall of humidity. I stand in front of my building second-guessing my choice to venture out. It is hot! I feel my phone vibrating in my purse. I reach my hand in my satchel and fish around for my phone. Found it. That is always a minor win when I can find my phone in my black hole of crap.

"Hello this is Lexi."

"Lexi, hey there, it's Nick."

"Hi Nick, how are you?"

"I am well. Listen Lexi any chance we can change our plans for tonight?"

"Sure," I say trying to disguise my disappointment.

"I don't want to completely cancel but something has come up at work so I was hoping you would be free for a make-up date on Friday?"

"Uh, sure. Friday works well."

"Great, how is seven?"

"Seven on Friday works."

"Cool. Then I will pick you up at seven. I have a little surprise so wear comfortable clothes."

I smile. "Ok, I look forward to it."

"Me too. Again, sorry about having to reschedule Lexi. But I can't wait for Friday."

I hang up the phone and am a little bummed out that I won't be seeing Nick tonight. Maybe my joke about the Vagina Monologues didn't go over too well. Or maybe I am overthinking things and the guy just has to work. I shove my phone back in my purse and begin my slow walk up to Newbury Street.

I was starving when I left my apartment, but this heat seems to have squelched my appetite. I stand outside of JP Licks and ponder the idea of ice cream for lunch. After careful consideration I decide a cold salad is the better choice. I look around Newbury Street as I contemplate the best place to grab a salad. The street is full of lunch seekers. I look across the street to Sonsie and see Ty. I am about to step off the sidewalk to intercept him when I see her.

I step back so both feet are securely on the sidewalk. She is breath taking. At first I didn't realize Ty was with her as he was a step behind her. But she turned and looked behind her and his face lit up. They approach the door to Sonsie and Ty steps up, opens the door and places his hand on the small of her back as he ushers her inside.

Huh. Well that must be the girl. I mean, of course it is the girl. She is exactly who Ty should be with. She is tall and well dressed. Her long hair is thick and dark. She looks good next to him. Good for him. I turn around and walk into JP Licks.

9

THE SECOND, SECOND DATE

Wednesday my alarm starts beeping at five thirty in the morning. I roll over and hit the snooze button. I play the snooze button game three more times and eventually pull myself out of bed. As I am washing my hair I realize I have a date with Patrick tonight. I really don't want to go. My mood is rather sullen this morning after seeing Ty with; whom I think is his new girl. The girl he really likes. "The one" I think is how he referenced her. My stomach turns. I wonder if it is too late to cancel my date with Patrick. I let the water wash over me as I try to come up with a valid excuse to cancel. I'm not very good at lying, people usually see right through my lies. Maybe I should just go out with him. Maybe it will be a good and needed distraction.

I start my day closing out the last details of the few open cases I still have. This is typically stuff I dislike doing, completing documentation on case files, going over receipts and submitting final bills. For some reason this morning, it is a painstakingly slow process. I am closing up a long chapter in my life. It is hard to let go of what I loved doing for so long. I don't have the emotional strength anymore to sit with people in such great pain.

I stare at the invoice records on my laptop screen. I have two outstanding invoices that are six months old and total $40,000.00. I have to resend these invoices each for the fourth time. The downside of working with people whose loved ones are facing embezzlement charges; they don't always have the money to pay their bills. However, they kept calling and kept using my services and I kept showing up to help each of these families. Unfortunately, I'm not in the position to call this work pro-bono and take a loss. I need this money. I need at least part of it. The upfront costs of my new business keep adding up to more and more. I have some padding but having these two invoices paid would just allow me to breathe a bit easier for a little longer. I send out the two invoices and provide monthly payment plans for each. Something is better than nothing.

I pour myself another cup of coffee and head out to have a smoke. I'm trying to stop thinking about my immediate worries, money and who the hell was that girl that Ty was with? The little nagging questions that are like thorns in my side. Outside I distract myself by observing everyone as they start to walk to work or to their summer class, a few runners, not a lot of smiling faces and I think about how lucky I am. I don't have to dredge down the same path day after day to work within the same four walls. I don't have to spend hours in traffic every day to do the same job. Oh wait, I will have to do all of that. I will be taking the same walk to the store day in and day out. I will be doing the same tasks; dealing with customers, marketing, making chocolate, day after day. I suddenly feel slightly panicked. Is this really what I want? Do I really want to settle down like this to the same routine day in and day out? Oh my, what if I have made the wrong choice? I try and calm myself down by reminding myself that with every change comes anxiety, with every job comes monotony. I have to remember how familiar and ordinary every airport and hotel room became to me. It was routine, just routine in different locations. I can do this.

I sip my coffee and gaze up into the mid-morning sunlight. I inhale the sun and feel its warmth on my face. Suddenly I got a chill. I opened my eyes and looked around, nothing odd, just the runners and people rushing off to work. I look around again just to be sure. I step out onto the sidewalk and look up. I look over to the building across the street and glance at the windows. I see one with a tall man wearing a black trench coat and he is looking down at me. He suddenly moves from the window. I wait and my eyes dart back and forth to the windows lined up next to the one he was standing in. Nothing. I wait another ten minutes. I wonder why anyone would be wearing a trench coat on such a gorgeous summer morning. And then I think, how disgusting, a flasher, but then he didn't flash me. Oh disgusting, he is a nasty peeper. Ugh, I need to go take a shower, with all of my shades shut. Gross!

As I get ready for my second date with Patrick I am well aware of a few things that are making me a bit uneasy. First, I have not actually dated in quite some time. Let alone, date two men at once. My prior lifestyle just never allowed me the time to really play the field shall we say and I did make a conscious choice to ease up on finding escape through dating. Second, I am burning the candle at both ends, and it is exhausting, something is going have to give shortly. Lastly, I am acutely aware that I am not putting in efforts in my "date preparation" to go out with Patrick. I argue with myself, which by the way, is much more difficult than having an argument with an actual person. I realize that I have had one date with Nick and just one with Patrick. I need to remember the last time I went out with Patrick I was ready to write him off and yet, had a surprisingly good time. However, actions speak louder than words, and if I am not putting the effort in, well, one needs to be honest and not lead anyone on. My counter argument, I have not slept with anyone. None of us owes anyone anything at this point except respect. If, after tonight I do not feel anything for Patrick then I will politely bow out. I mean really, who is to say they are not both playing the field as well. Actually, I know Patrick is.

Ugh. All of these thoughts have been spinning around in my head for most of the day. I don't know how people do it, date multiple people, work, friends. And the games, oh, I hate the dating games.

Patrick picks me up at 7:30 p.m. I am wearing a little white tank top dress and a cute pair of sling back red heals, my hair is pulled back in a ponytail as the night is hot and the city air still thick from the high humidity. I pop out from my building and there is Patrick, standing on the sidewalk next to his car. He greets me with a kiss on the cheek and a "wow, you look great!" as he opens the passenger door for me and I jump in. As Patrick walks around to the driver's side, I can't help but think he and Nick went to the same stellar school of chivalry. Stop Lexi; you cannot compare these two men. Patrick gets into the car and turns to me with a huge grin on his face, his eyes wide.

"What?" I ask?

Patrick shakes his head, "Nothing, you just really do look great. It's nice to see you."

"Well, thank you. I'm glad we have a chance to go out again."

Patrick takes a right off Beacon Street and gets onto Storrow Drive. "Where are we headed?" I ask.

Patrick turns to me and smiles and then he shifts his eyes back to the road. His takes just a bit too long to answer me. It is just long enough for me to wonder if he is not sure where we are going, did not hear me, or if he is stoned. Patrick clears his throat.

"Finally," I think to myself.

"I thought since it is such a hot evening, it might be nice to head to Marina Bay for dinner."

"Great! I love Marina Bay."

Marina Bay, as usual for a hot summer night was very busy. Patrick made reservations at Siros a great Italian restaurant overlooking the marina. We were seated at an outdoor table with the perfect view to watch all of the people strolling by on the boardwalk. Patrick and I quickly discovered that we had an equal love of people watching. Who doesn't really? It is so fun to sit in a crowded place and watch people walk by. It's as if you are watching life walk right by your dinner table; the lovers who hold hands and stroll slowly, the awkward first dates walking side by side unsure of what to do with their hands, the friends who have all had too much to drink, too much sun and speaking much too loudly, and the parents mindlessly dragging screaming kids while gazing longingly at our table for two.

Patrick and I laugh with each other while we try and create the best stories to go along with those who pass by our table. I learn a bit more about Patrick this time around. He is an avid runner, enjoys golf, and is quite committed to his work. I discover he married young. He is divorced but does not have any children. I press him a bit about his divorce. Mostly I just want to know if he has passed the two-year mark. He has not.

"So let me try to get the timing down. You met your wife in college. You were married by the age of 25. You stayed married for nine years, which is impressive. And you don't have any children." I pause to gauge Patrick's reaction.

Patrick grins in amusement, "yes."

"And you finalized your divorce two months ago; however, you were separated for six months prior to that. So all total you and your wife have been apart for eight months."

Patrick just grins at me. Again, he stares for an uncomfortably long time. I will give him a pass on this awkward stare as my summary of the last 14 years of his life had as much emotion tied to it as a third grade word problem. Patrick finally lets out a deep sigh. I am starting to see his pattern here, long silence while staring blankly at you, deep sigh or a throat clearing, and then words.

"Yes." That is all he says.

That should be all I need.

"Let's walk." Patrick says.

Patrick and I strolled along the boardwalk of Marina Bay. He held my hand, and we discussed lighter topics. I struggled though. We no longer had the entertainment of outsiders and I noticed the conversation was getting harder and harder. It was uncomfortable. He suddenly seemed awkward and tense. The sun had set but the boardwalk had its own lights and the evening was warm and romantic under any circumstances. Patrick suddenly stopped and pulled me close to him. He wrapped his arms around me and just hugged me tightly. He pulled back from me a bit and kissed me. I would like to tell you that this was an amazing mind blowing kiss that negated all prior awkward moments we had that evening. But I can't. It was the most uncomfortable kiss I have ever had. He pressed his lips on to mine; tightly closed, and stood there. Well, technically we stood there: lip to lip; pressed together, and that is it. I almost wanted to start talking with our lips pressed together. I was waiting for something, anything, but nothing. He finally, after what felt like ten minutes pulled away, stared at me and smiled. He then grabbed my hand and we started walking back to the car. I wanted to look around and see if there was a camera crew somewhere. Were my friends pranking me? Did this guy think that was a kiss?

I stayed distracted for the twenty-five-minute ride home by discussing the large checklist of things I had to get done before the opening of my truffle shop. Patrick seemed genuinely interested as he had launched a business and was quite knowledgeable about the process. He even offered quite a few helpful tips that I had not even considered. I somehow avoided another awkward, ten-minute lip press and got away with just a hug and "yes, let's do it again." All I could think of when I got into the safety of my own apartment was *what the hell was that?* And *wait until Ty hears this one. And why did I agree to go out with him again?* I hate that about myself. I have a hard time saying no, even when I know there is no way I want to do something. It's like I'm afraid that the person in front of me will just shatter if I say no. Or worse, they won't like me. It's so messed up, my people pleasing co-dependent craziness. So instead of just politely bowing out I prolong the inevitable, and typically make matters worse, by agreeing to something I don't want to do. Respect Lexi, you need to give this man respect. You need to bow out, tell him why you are bowing out, and leave it be.

10

Friday finally rolls around. I'm so excited I get up before my alarm goes off. I can't even pretend to be cool or casual at this point. I can't wait to see Nick tonight I don't think my jam-packed day will go by quickly enough. I have scheduled my day to do all of my work in the morning. At noon I'm getting my haircut and highlighted, then on to the manicure, pedicure, wax. Yes, that is right I'm getting a wax. Now, I am not sure if I'm going to have sex with Nick tonight but I like to be prepared for all possibilities. Truth be told, I am actively trying to will myself to not have sex with him. It is only our second date! It's hard. I am so darn attracted to the man. However, I also quite like him. He is smart, nice, and seems to have his act together. And did I mention he is hot. And God the man can kiss. If his kiss is any indication of his other talents, I'm in real trouble, super-duper knock your socks off trouble. And yes, I did just say super-duper. I'm in the corny lustful state. My phone beeps and it is a text from Nick:

> *Good Morning Lexi. I have a very busy day today, but I can't wait to see you tonight. I haven't stopped thinking about you. I will meet you at your place at seven.*

I smile a huge grin and plop on my couch. My whole body is tingling as I read and re-read his text. How am I going to get any work done today? I finally get my head together and send back a text to Nick.

I'm looking forward to seeing you. Don't let work tire you out!

I reluctantly sit at my desk for three hours. The only thing I accomplished was some great daydreaming about Nick. Daydreaming, whoever came up with that word is brilliant. The problem with having your own business is that it never goes away. So on the days, like today, when I am totally unproductive, I rationalize by thinking it's not a big deal because it will still be here tomorrow. I decided to call it quits and head out for my day of beauty.

I justify my day of beauty and the money I am spending with the knowledge that I'm not going to have a lot of opportunity for these kinds of luxurious activities come September. What am I getting myself into? August is the calm before the storm. I have basically done everything I can do for my new business until September. I'm no longer taking on new clients for my current business so that is in the 'wrap up' stage. I should be enjoying this time but I just have a nagging feeling like I should be doing something so it's hard to relax. It's similar to when I first moved to Los Angeles. It was an odd feeling to be a life-long east coaster and then move to the West Coast and be three hours behind everyone I knew. I felt like the rabbit in Alice in Wonderland. I always had a feeling that I was late but I didn't know what I was late for. That is how I feel now, I feel like there must be one hundred things I should be doing, but I do not know what they are. It is very unnerving.

When I finish my afternoon of beauty I am feeling much more relaxed. I mean really is there anything better than getting your hair washed. The massage they give you while washing your hair is just fantastic. I'm not a fan of full body massages. They hurt. I'm rather high-strung and with all of my running around airports in high heels, my body is just tense. I know that the point of a massage is to work the tension out of your body, but it hurts so much the first time that I can never be consistent. But, as for a head massage, that is something I could do daily.

I leave my salon and head down Newbury Street towards home. I take my time as it is a beautiful late afternoon and I am feeling like a million bucks. As I wait at the light to cross over Dartmouth Street, daydreaming again, I hear, "Hi Lexi," whispered from behind me. It scared the heck out of me; I stopped myself from grabbing a hold of the guy in front of me.

"Whoa, sorry, I didn't mean to scare you."

I turned around to see Patrick standing behind me with a very concerned look on his face.

"Patrick," I whisper, as I finally am able to breathe again. There goes my relaxed, Zen feeling.

"I am really sorry Lexi; I didn't mean to scare you."

"No, it's fine. I was totally spacing out. How are you?"

"I'm great. I just finished a meeting and was going to grab a cup of coffee before I head back downtown. Do you want to join me?" Patrick asked.

"Oh, I would love to, but I have to get back to work as well."

"Well, how about if we just walk together? I have something I need to talk to you about." Patrick asked.

"Sure."

"Let's get off this street. The crowds are not very good for conversation." Patrick says as points us down Dartmouth Street towards Commonwealth Ave.

I followed alongside of him. All the while wondering what is so important to discuss as I just saw him two days ago. We end up sitting on a wooden bench along the Commonwealth Ave Mall. Patrick inhales deeply and then looks at me but does not say anything. He looks like he is about to speak but he just stares at me, sort of like his kissing without actually kissing. I count to ten silently in my head, reminding myself that he is the one who wanted to talk to me; I do not need to start this conversation.

"Lexi, I am not sure how to say this so I am just going to say it."

"Okay," I reply slowly.

Patrick takes another deep breath. "I was not completely honest with you. I'm actually not divorced from my wife; we are just separated."

Well now that's unexpected. It looks like the universe just gave me the easiest get out of jail free card. Before I even have time to say anything, Patrick puts his hand on my knee and looks at me with puppy dog eyes and says, "I'm really sorry Lexi. I didn't mean to hurt you in anyway. I mean, I know we really connected and that kiss the other night. Wow. I'm sorry I lied Lexi."

I take a look around for the hidden cameras. This guy has got to be kidding. I quickly come to my senses and realize the universe is not just giving me a get out jail free card, it is also giving me a run for your life now card. Patrick begins to speak again and I put my hand up to let him know it is my turn. He tilts his head and gives me a pouty look by sticking out his lower lip. Now I feel like this is getting really strange.

"Patrick, we went out twice and had a very nice time. Although I do not know why you lied, that is not my business. I appreciate you telling me that you are married and well, I hope you and your wife work it out."

"Lexi, I feel so guilty. I mean I led you on. I am just taken with you. I've never felt such a strong connection to someone."

I think to myself, *Dude you are married. I hope you feel more connected to your wife.* "Patrick, we went on two dates. I'm fine. Again, I hope things work out for you and your wife." I stress the word 'wife'. He seems to be forgetting that he is married.

"Well, you don't seem very broken up. I guess the feelings weren't mutual." Patrick responds with a snarky tone of voice.

"Patrick you are married. I wish you well. I am going to leave now." I begin to stand up to go and Patrick grabs my arm. I don't say a word I just glare at him and he quickly releases his hold on my arm.

"I am sorry." Patrick says as he puts his arms up as if to surrender.

I glare for a bit longer and he hangs his head in defeat. I turn and walk away.

I walk down the Commonwealth Ave path until I hit Exeter Street. I head up Exeter to get back to Newbury. I need to feel the safety of the crowds on Newbury. I keep thinking how thoroughly screwed up this situation is. The guy is bizarre. I could feel the adrenaline pulsing through my body. Although I knew I was not in any real danger, it is still unnerving to have someone put their hands on you. If there is anything I have learned from my past, it's that not everyone is as nice as they may appear. You may think you know someone, but unless you are listening to the thoughts in their head, you have no idea who they are or what they may be capable of.

I need a night with my girls. They are going to love this story. I pull out my IPhone and quickly send a group text to see if we can all get together soon. I stop before I cross over Fairfield and look behind me to be sure a car isn't going to run me over when they turn left onto Fairfield. As I glance over my shoulder, I see him. It is the exact same experience as I had when I walked out of Stephanie's after dinner with all of my friends, and again on the Mass Ave Bridge. I feel cool air around me. It feels like time is slowing down. He had a baseball cap and sunglasses on, but it was him. I don't know how I know this, I don't know why I know this, I just do. A car honks and snaps me out of my spell. I look at the driver and he roughly waves his hand to signal me to cross the street. I wave him by. I look back across the street and the stranger is gone. I dart across Newbury before the next wave of cars come my way. I look in both directions but there is no sign of him.

I debate going into the CVS that I am standing in front of or just wait to see if he comes out, if he's even in there. Where else could he go? The homeless guy who always sits on a milk crate in front of the CVS and sings songs about the people walking by starts singing, "Will you give me money, pretty blonde girl who looks like she just saw a ghost?"

I just look at the homeless guy and laugh. I pull out a dollar, stick it in his coffee can and ask, "did you see him?"

"Thank you ghost chasing blonde girl." The homeless guy sings to me.

The Newbury street pedestrians walk by us giving us both equally peculiar stares. Neither one of us seems to care. The homeless guy keeps singing about the people passing by and I keep looking in the crowds for my ghost.

I finally give up my search and start walking home. I wonder if I'm just being paranoid. Maybe he is just a creepy looking guy who lives around here and I happen to notice him a few times. I have gut feelings though and they are usually correct. I don't always know it at the time, but I feel it. And I feel something. Something is off. It feels like when I first met Alistair. A chill runs down my spine. I can't even think of Alistair without getting the creeps. The scariest most sinister person I have ever come in contact with. I get a bigger chill this time, so much so that my shoulders flinch backwards. *Back in the box Lexi, stuff it all back into the box.*

A text message came to my phone promptly at seven in the evening. It was from Nick and it read, *I am here whenever you are ready.* I let out a huge sigh of relief. Because of the crazy happenings of the day, I found myself holding my breath hoping that Nick wouldn't cancel on me. I grabbed my keys and my purse and ran out the door. I had to do some deep breathing in the elevator to calm myself down. I realize that having been worried about him not showing up made me just a little too over-joyed that he had. This is only our second date; I still need to play it cool. I walked out of my building to see Nick standing on the street wearing pair of dark jeans, a tee shirt and a backpack resting on one shoulder. He looked hotter than ever. He stood there smiling at me as I walked up the stairs to the street. His smile got bigger as I approached him. He didn't say anything, he kept his eyes focused in on mine, and he gently grabbed my face with one hand and kissed me. I felt his mouth open and his tongue search for mine. *Desire, a good chill, a real kiss, thank you.*

Nick released my lips from his and whispered in my ear, "you look beautiful and you taste even better."

More desire, a bigger chill, weak in the knees, I think I am in love.

"Well," I begin as I try to speak without falling over my words, "you bring jeans and a tee-shirt to a whole new level."

Nick laughed. "I'm glad you approve."

"So what's in the backpack?"

"A surprise." Nick said as he grabbed my hand and led me down Beacon Street towards Mass Ave.

Nick and I saunter down to the Esplanade and made our way to one of the docks along the Charles. Nick plopped down his backpack and pulled out a plush blanket. He then pulled out a brown bag and put it off to the side. Next, a plastic container he opened that contained strawberries and grapes. Another container was extracted filled with cheese and crackers, and then a small bottle of grape juice that he put off to the side. For the grand finale, Nick pulled out two wine glasses and a bottle of Opus One.

"Wow, now that is an impressive picnic. But what's the grape juice for?" I ask eyeing all of the goods.

"Just a cover in case one of Boston's finest decides to question the contents of our glasses. I would hate to waste a bottle of Opus."

"Good thinking! And may I ask what's in the brown bag?"

"Ah, the best part, a chicken parm sub in case we get really hungry."

I smile, kneel down next to Nick, wrap my arms around his neck and kiss him. "Thank you, this is awesome."

We chatted and ate food and drank an amazing bottle of wine. I just kept feeling more and more connected to him as the night and conversation moved forward.

"Lexi, this is the most fun I have had in a long time. I really, really like you. But, there is something I have to tell you."

I could feel my face fall. I think my heart just skipped a beat. "You're married." I blurt out.

Nick looked at me confused. "What, no. I'm not married." He let out a slight chuckle and hung his head. He reached for my hand and gently caressed my fingers. "I think I mentioned I had a busy day at work. And, I, uh," he stumbled searching for words, "I want to spend the night with you."

Ok that is not so bad I thought to myself. I gave him a confused look, as I was confused. "Hmm, I thought you were going to give me some bad news."

Nick smiled a soft smile, still holding my hand, "Well, that is not all of it. I found out today that I have a significant opportunity."

My heart sank.

"I have been offered the opportunity to open our Seattle office."

"As in Washington?"

"Yes."

"Wow, congratulations. That is fantastic." I said in such a fashion as anyone would who is supposed to be happy for someone even though they are completely breaking up inside.

"Thank you. It's, well, it is what I have wanted for a long time. I didn't see it coming. It has been pushed aside and pushed aside for so many years I thought it was dead in the water."

"But it is alive?"

"It is."

"And you are going."

"I am."

"When?"

Nick took a deep breath. "Two weeks."

I let out a huge sullen sigh. I think my heart just broke. I gave Nick a soft smile. I curled my knees up to my chest, wrapped my arms around my legs and put my head down. I want to cry. This hurts. This sucks. After a few moments I pick my head up and rest my chin on my knees. "Well that sucks."

Nick smiles. "You know I hear they are in dire need of a boutique truffle shop in Seattle."

I smile. It is safe for him to say that, knowing I will never go. It is safe for me to love hearing it, knowing he is going to go. Nick wraps his arm around me and I snuggle into his shoulder. We sat and stared out onto the Charles. We eventually packed up and slowly made our way towards my apartment, holding hands and stopping to kiss every so often. When we reach my building Nick stops short of the entryway and pulls me towards him. He gives me yet another sensual kiss.

"I am going to miss those," I say, still wrapped in his embrace.

"Hmm. I guess spending the night is out of the question." Nick raises an eyebrow to signal questionable hope.

"Yes. Unfortunately, it is. I don't think I could handle it. Well, I couldn't handle the aftermath anyway."

Nick kisses me again. "Stay in touch?"

"Absolutely. I wish you luck random hot guy."

Nick gives me a confused look.

"It was what I called you before I actually knew your name."

Nick gives me a big hug. "Am I going to regret this Lexi?"

"You won't."

Nick motions for me to walk into my building. "I'm not leaving until you are safely behind those doors.

I walk into my building and do not turn around. I can feel my eyes welling up with tears. I get into my apartment and flop down on the couch. I cry a little. I really liked him. "What the fuck universe," I whisper as I kick my heels against the sofa cushions.

This has been the most bizarre day. There I was thinking Patrick was crazy because he reacted so strongly after only two dates. And here I am, crying after a second. Patrick is crazy though. He is friggin' married. I will give myself tonight, tonight and maybe tomorrow. I can be sad about Nick until tomorrow night, and then it is over. And no more dating until my business is up and running.

The next morning, as with every morning the sun rose. It's funny to think about, no matter what is going on in your life, no matter how important you think you are, the sun is going to do what it needs to do, regardless of you. The sun is going to rise and the sun is going to set; what you chose to do with the time between those events is really up to you. Today, I chose lunch with the girls. There is really no better way to mend your mood than hanging with your closest friends. They love with you, they despise with you, they laugh with you, and they cry with you. It is truly co-dependency in its grandest form.

11

A DAY OF MIXED EMOTIONS

I walk into Jackie's office promptly at 8:30 a.m. I feel as though it's Friday not Monday. My energy is just sapped and I did not get my Sunday with Ty as he is out of town on business. At least that is what he told me. He could have been out of town with his "It Girl".

"Good morning Lexi." Jackie says as I walk into her office. She comes around from her desk and gives me my weekly Monday morning hug. "How was your week?"

"Interesting." I reply very matter of fact. We take our usual seats and I continue. "Remember when you told me that I was a survivor?"

"Yes." Jackie replies and says nothing more as she knows there is more coming.

"I agree with you. I am a survivor and it's fucking exhausting Jackie." I pause there are so many things I want and need to say. "I survived when my parents died. I survived when my grandparents died. I have survived heartache. I survived the guilt when I ran away from my impending nuptials. But I am exhausted."

"Are you exhausted from surviving or running?"

"Both.

"And now, you have decided to stay in one spot, and open a new business. I guess you are still running just in place." Jackie points out.

"Yes."

"Are you feeling an urge to run away?"

"Yes." I say, as that is true. "I feel a strong urge to want to change my scenery."

"Why?"

"I don't know." I say, still being honest.

"You know Lexi I find it interesting that the only time you mentioned guilt was when you talked about running away from your fiancé." Jackie replies.

"Well, the guilt was overwhelming."

"Hmm. More so than being in the same car accident as your parents and only you survived? More so than not being able to see your grandparents the year before they died?" Jackie pauses. "More so than Ashley?"

I just buried my face in my hands and started crying. The guilt in my life is killing me. I'm not surviving. I'm dying. I pull myself together and grab some tissues. I kept thinking to myself, *I have to do this. I have to.*

"Just tell me about her, not what happened." Jackie says softly.

"Okay." I replied.

"Take your time Lex."

"Where do I start?"

"Try the beginning."

I chuckled. I appreciate Jackie's quick wit. "I had been in Los Angeles about six months. I was struggling. I was trying to deal with the aftermath of my decision to not get married. I was alone. I knew three people. I was just really lonely. I traveled to meet with my clients, in their homes or at hotels and I interacted with people on the phone, but for the most part if I wasn't with a client I was working from my apartment, by myself. I didn't have the usual organic ways to meet people. I wasn't in an office so I didn't have that connection with anyone. I didn't go to college there or have any real friends there to help expand my social circle. It was an isolating and difficult time.

One day I was watching this talk show and a young actress was talking about her struggles moving to Los Angeles. I remember being enthralled with the story. She said she was so lonely until she met a friend in acting class and they became best buddies. She said it changed her entire outlook on Los Angeles. She then turned to the camera as if to be speaking to me and said, 'for all of you struggling women, just wait, once you meet your best girl, life will get better.' I thought great, but how the heck am I going to meet any girlfriends.

I began to force myself to work from a coffee shop around the corner from my house for at least a few hours a day. It took me twice as long to get stuff done, but at least I wasn't isolated. There was a woman who worked there who seemed to be about my age. We would exchange pleasantries and certainly became familiar acquaintances. One day I was there after her shift ended and she asked to sit down with me. It turned out that she was two years older than I and lived two streets away from me. She was an actress and getting some small parts. She was making enough money but she did the coffee shop gig to stay connected and not feel isolated. That's how I met Ashley."

"So you met her unexpectedly, like how you meet the men in your life." Jackie replied.

"Yes, exactly." I laughed.

"So what was she like?" Jackie inquired.

"Well, she was, unexpected, if I can use your phrase. She was dynamic and smart. She grew up in the mid-west. We both despised seafood. We had a lot in common, but we were different."

"How so?"

"Well, she had this sense of adventure."

"Most would say you do too Lexi."

"True, but hers was more free. I do things that many people might be afraid to do. I look like I take chances but I always have some sort of plan and a backup plan. She was more of a free spirit. She was responsible, paid her bills, and showed up when she needed to, but it's hard to explain. I have a laundry list of fun things I want to do. If we were talking and I said that I have always wanted to go take dance lessons, she would show up the next day with a dance lesson schedule. I guess she worked hard and played hard. She knew how to have fun and enjoy life. She helped me enjoy my life more." I smiled thinking about Ashley. *God I miss her.*

"You miss her." Jackie stated

"I do."

"Where does the guilt come from Lexi?"

Jackie, this is as far as we can go. I'm not ready to talk about that. It is time to put me back together again. I have a function."

"Okay," Jackie agrees. "Guided meditation?"

"Yes, please." *Back in the box, Lexi. It all goes back in the box.*

I left Jackie's office feeling tired. It was hard to speak about Ashley and even harder to put my thoughts of her away in a box. Jackie's office is in Beacon Hill, I basically leave my apartment and walk ten blocks up Beacon Street to get there; however, on the way home I decide to cut through the Public Garden and take in the summer beauty. The Public Garden is breathtaking and serene. It was too peaceful, too quiet, too pretty. What the hell was I thinking? I am trying to shove memories in a box, I don't need quiet, and I need chaos. I exit the Public Garden, cross over Arlington Street and head down Newbury. It is just what I needed. Crowds of people exiting the T-stops, cars honking, window-shopping galore; it was just one distraction after another. Perfect.

Halfway down Newbury Street my mind is far from therapy and already running through my list of the one hundred things I have to get done today. I remember I need paper for my printer so I quickly cut across Newbury Street when there was a break in the traffic. As I am walking up to the CVS, I hear my favorite homeless guy singing to me. "Do you have some money jay-walking blonde girl, will you help me pretty jay-walker."

Seriously, I don't know how he does it, he wasn't even looking at me, how does he know I jaywalked? I pull some change out of my pocket and put it in his can while asking, "How did you even see me?"

I don't know why I bother to ask; he never answers me. I head into CVS and grab a ream of paper, a bottle of water, and some goldfish crackers. I shouldn't buy the goldfish, as I know I will eat the whole bag, but I buy them anyway. I decide I will go all out and stop at Starbucks for a peppermint latte to wash down the goldfish. Breakfast of champions my friends; don't judge me and I won't judge you. I head out of the store and walk by my singing homeless man. One of the things I love about him, if you give him money, he won't sing to you twice; well, at least not for a few hours. I was about to step off the curb to cross to the next block and I suddenly got goose bumps. I stepped back on to the curb to be sure I didn't miss a car running a stop sign. Those Boston drivers are not to be trusted. I don't see any cars so I step off the curb and I hear, "Ghosts among us. Ghosts, Ghosts, Ghosts, Ghosts." I freeze.

I turn around and the singing homeless man is not looking at me. I take six steps to get back to him, looking around everywhere. "Hey, were you talking to me?" I whisper.

The singing homeless guy doesn't look at me; he is looking away from me down the street. I keep looking around and I do not see anyone. I am so frustrated! I pull a five-dollar bill out of my back pocket; the change that I was too lazy to put into my wallet from my CVS purchase. I place it into his bucket and whisper, "keep singing to me." A girl carrying a large instrument case is walking toward him and he sings, "music girl, music girl, will you help me music girl." She keeps walking. I sigh and start walking towards Starbucks, all the while my eyes are wide-open scanning both sides of Newbury Street. He either really sees something or he sees me as a total sucker. Right now I am thinking the latter. Shit. He never sings to you back to back. He is so aware. He sees everything and you don't even know he is looking. He knows who gives him money. He never sings twice. What the hell is going on?

I start walking faster. I get to the Starbucks and the line is huge. Of course it is. Looks like coffee at home and goldfish. I don't have time for this. I don't have time for Starbucks, or dating. I don't have time for dealing with the ghosts from my past or my present. And I certainly don't have time for some singing homeless guy who is probably just messing with me. The universe is messing with me, and I don't find it funny.

I get to the bottom of Mass Ave and I slow my pace. I impatiently wait for a break in the stream of cars so that I can yet again jaywalk across Beacon Street and get over to my building. My phone has been buzzing like mad in my purse; but I am not in the mood to answer it. God I am in a bad mood; it must be PMS.

I finally get into the safety of my own apartment; I make coffee and rip into my goldfish. I don't think I can get them into my mouth fast enough. These things are so addictive. It is only ten thirty in the morning and I am already in such a funk. Maybe therapy first thing on a Monday is not such a good idea. I feel like I just need to crawl back into bed, pull my covers over my head and start over tomorrow. If only. I grab my phone out of my city satchel and see that I have two missed calls from Nick. Nick? And a text from him reading: *Hey Lexi, time to speak today?* Maybe my day will get better. Maybe he is calling because he went to work on Monday morning and his company decided to not open the Seattle office. The way my day is going I highly doubt that is the news I am going to hear, but a girl can hope.

I returned Nick's phone call and I was very wrong. Not only is he going to Seattle but he is leaving in two days. He wants me to come by tonight as he says he has something to give me. Now my stronger side would say thank you but no thank you. Unfortunately, today, that side of me is not coming through. Today my crazy, emotional, irrational side is prevailing and I said yes. What good could possibly come from me going to see a man, who I had a huge crush on, and who is leaving in two days to go across the country for an indefinite amount of time?

I manage to get through the rest of my day without hurting anyone by playing solitaire on my computer and eating mindlessly. It is nearly five in the afternoon and I am supposed to meet Nick at his place at five. I am going to be late, and I do not really care. That is exactly the adolescent mood I am in right now. I am a bit angry and rather passive aggressive. I have got to snap out of this.

I had never been to Nick's place but it turns out he lives about eight blocks away on Commonwealth Avenue. It is a good-sized building.   Nick buzzes me in and I head up the wide staircase.   He is waiting at the top of the stairs outside his apartment door.   And of course looking as handsome as ever in jeans and a tee shirt.   Why am I into torturing myself today?

"Hi" Nick says as he wraps his arms around me to give me a hug. He even smells amazing.

"Hi, so this is your place?"

"This is it, come on in. Pardon the mess."   Nick holds the door and let me head in first.

Nick leads me around his apartment. His is one of a few on the top two floors of his building. It is a nice open-concept first floor and two bedrooms upstairs. We then head up one more flight of stairs and walk out to a rooftop deck.   It is his deck but surrounded by three other rooftop decks, one adjacent to his and two behind him. All of the deck owners have managed to create some privacy, yet not lose their views of the Back Bay by using small potted trees and decking lattice. Nick has a plate of fruit and cheese laid out on a table and a bottle of wine with two glasses.

"Wow, Nick, this is amazing." I say as I take in the view.

"Thank you. It is hard to give up."

"I bet."

"Here, let's sit. I thought maybe we could have a one last glass of wine before my departure." Nick says as he leads me over to the table with the wine and seats me on one of the four comfortably cushioned, wooden lounge chairs.   The deck furniture reminds me of the stuff you find in the lounge area of swanky west coast hotels.

"Thank you. This is beautiful. All you need is a fire pit." I jest.

"If I thought I could get away with it Lexi; I would have one."

Nick pours each of us a glass of wine and then sits in the chair next to me. "Lexi, thanks for coming over. I guess I panicked a bit when I found out I was leaving so soon. I wanted to say I was sorry for all of this. I know it is not my fault, but the timing really sucks. I was hoping to spend I don't know a lot of time with you, an indefinite amount of time with you. I was looking forward to really getting to know you. And I am sorry that can't happen."

I feel like crying. "Thank you Nick. I appreciate that. I too was looking forward to getting to know you and I know this wasn't planned or foreseen by you in anyway. I get how corporate America works. I don't particularly like it right now, but I get it."

"See right there. Your honesty and understanding makes me want to hang out with you even more. You're quite a catch Lexi, I hope you know that."

"Thanks."

"So, I have something for you." Nick hands me an envelope.

I give him a curious look and open it. It is a letter requesting 1000 twelve-piece truffle gift boxes to be sent to Seattle by November 15th. I had to read it twice. "ONE THOUSAND?? Nick?"

"You can handle that right?" Nick asks in his best business voice.

I am dumbfounded. I am not sure how to respond. I'm not sure I can handle it. "One thousand twelve packs that is what you are requesting?"

"Yes."

"Nick, do you have any idea how much that is going to cost you?"

"Well," Nick hesitates, "I have a good idea. Lexi you gave me your website address, so I looked it up. I think it is going to cost me somewhere around $25,000.00 plus shipping I assume."

"Yes. Nick, but you haven't even tried them? This is a lot of money."

"I need holiday gifts for my clients Lexi. Are you trying to talk me out of a $25,000.00 sale for you?" Nick asks, trying to shed some light on my poor sales tactics.

"No, no I am not."

"Good, because I wanted to be your first big order." Nick says with a big grin. "And it's a perfect link me opening up the new office in Seattle as you open up your new store in Boston. I'm hoping our Seattle clients will enjoy the Boston flare." He picks up his wine glass and motions for me to do the same. "To our success Lexi."

"To our success! Thank you."

We finish our wine and decide it's time to part ways. As Nick is walking me out of his apartment I stop to glance at a picture of him and his friends at a golf outing. I had to take a closer look at the picture to find Nick, my eyes looked over a man standing next to him and I got a shiver.

"Oh, Lexi, get a chill?" Nick asks as he sees my shoulders shudder.

"I guess, who is that next to you? The bald guy?"

"Oh that's Richard, lifelong friend. That picture was taken in Myrtle Beach. We do an annual golf trip. One of the four times a year I actually play."

"Hmm. Cute picture. Sorry, I guess your friend Richard gives me the chills, not in a good way."

"Good, because if I can't be with you, I certainly don't want anyone I know with you." Nick jokes. "He's harmless, married with children."

I smile at Nick although from my physical reaction I'm not convinced about the harmless part. He looks familiar, but I can't place him. "He must just remind me of someone." I finally respond.

I make my way home not sure about how or what I am feeling. I am sullen, anxious, grateful, and confused. Will I miss Nick or will I just miss the idea of what it could have been with Nick? Probably a little of both. I had a weird day filled with frustrations and little work done; yet, I have in my city satchel an order worth $25,000.00. I am insanely grateful for the order. The store isn't even open yet and I'm making money. Who is that lucky? I should be doing a happy dance but instead I'm completely panicked about getting 12,000 truffles made, boxed, and delivered to Seattle by November fifteenth. This is a serious order. He's counting on me. Is Nick really that nice, that awesome that he spends $25000.00 on truffles he hasn't even tasted? Sure it's his company's money but he is taking the risk. Damn, what a complete bummer he's leaving. I think I could eat 12,000 truffles right now. And that guy Richard, who is he and why did his picture give me the creeps? I just need to get home and go to bed and forget this day ever happened. Well, except for my large order. I can't forget about that.

PART 2

12

I BROKE A GLASS

September 1, 2015, is change day in Boston. I think I mentioned how the City of Boston seems to double in size when all of the college students come back into town. The onslaught of students happens slowly at first, it is almost unnoticeable, like the days getting shorter in July. That is how the college students begin to seep into the city in August. It is a slow process, first the returning kids who sub-leased their apartments for a summer stint. The athletes are next as they have practice to attend. The freshman slowly begin to migrate into the dorms and then, before you know it's September first.

Boston is a city that relies heavily on its colleges and universities. The rental market is no different. Actually ninety percent of the rental market completely revolves around the academic year. The majority of leases, whether they are for college kids or not, begin on September first and end on August thirty-first. Thousands upon thousands of people move on the same day. It is utter chaos. The Back Bay streets are nearly impassable and to attempt to get into the Fenway area is risking all of your patience let alone your actual cardiac health. The tiny streets of Boston are packed with U-Haul's, giant SUV's, moving vans, station wagons, you name it and they are all double and triple parked. The grocery store aisles are jammed, the sidewalks are gridlocked, there is trash everywhere, and forget about trying to get a reservation or takeout. As a resident, if you are lucky enough to not have to move, you have to decide early, either you leave for a few days, or you hunker down with all the food and supplies you need for at least forty-eight hours.

Under normal circumstances, I would flee the city for a few days, but this year, with just weeks to go before I open my business, I did not have the luxury of time on my side. And this year it is a Tuesday, a normal work day for those whose lives do not revolve around the colleges and universities. It is a big Tuesday for me; the construction is starting today. My truffle shop design will finally begin to take shape. The storefront is actually quite simple. It is not a coffee shop or a place where people would gather and hang out. My storefront is there for me to display the goods, people to purchase them and move on their way. The storefront is not where I expect to make most of my money. Yes, I will have gift boxes and individual truffles to buy but it is really there to showcase the goods and encourage the larger orders for parties, holiday gifts, weddings, and the corporate gifts. The storefront is designed to encourage a shopper to taste how amazing these truffles are and to showcase the beautiful delivery everyone wants for their parties and gifts. There will be sample gift displays but nothing is pre-packaged every thing is made to order or be purchased from the current supplies. The bigger issue is the kitchen. We are completely tearing everything out and starting from scratch. The kitchen needs to be up to code for the state and the city.

My construction crew consists of two guys who come highly recommended by Ty. They have agreed to work on my small project, make everything perfect, up to code, and done within three weeks. I know, because Ty recommended them, and because Ty gives them most of their work leads right now, they will do a good job. However, I need everything to be perfect. I need everything to be done in two weeks. I have a large order to fill and I am running low on money too. So, because of that, I am up early and waiting in line at Dunkin Donuts. I will do just about anything to keep these guys happy and working.

The guys were glad to have me show up with coffee and food. They set up quickly and got right to work. I went back to my apartment to do my own work without the dust or noise. I brought them lunch and then went back again at four-thirty in the afternoon right as they were wrapping up. The guys left and I stayed in the shop to just look around. This is technically the first full day it has been mine. I am freaking out and completely excited, all at the same time. I can't believe this is finally happening. The signing of the lease was a big deal but I still had to wait just over a month before I could get the keys. Now I'm here. In a month, if all goes well this place will look more like the vision I have in my head. I walk around the tiny storefront and smile. Fortunately for me the guys covered the windows with paper so no one on the street could actually see me walking around a dusty room with a Cheshire cat grin on my face.

The rest of the week consisted of the same routine for me. I would rise early and be one of the first in line at Dunkin Donuts. I would head over to the shop meet the guys and go over what was happening for the day. I would pop in at lunch with their orders they had given me that morning and then back again at the end of the day to see the progress. Things were moving along nicely. The guys were working on Saturday and I set up my mobile office at a coffee shop across the street. I lined up fifteen interviews for Saturday. I need two part-time employees, whose primary functions will be the working in the storefront, accommodating customer orders, working the cash register, and filling larger pre-orders. I need people who will be willing to fill boxes with four, twelve, and fifteen truffles. I need people who will pay attention to detail when placing truffles in containers, on trays, or wrapping things up with pretty bows. And, I need one full-time employee who will be my assistant. They will truly be the one I rely on the most. I will need to teach them how to do everything, which is going to be tough as I am not sure I even know how to do everything.

By the end of a long day on Saturday my head was spinning. I had met all kinds of people that day. I interviewed some people who had absolutely zero experience, one guy who was missing a few teeth, and a girl who kept apologizing every time her phone beeped but yet still checked it and never turned it off. The highlight of my day was when I was able to hire a part-time employee. She had worked for three summers in a cupcake shop, she is a full-time college student who is paying her own way through school, and the best part, she wants to work nights and weekends. Her name is Sally and she accepted my offer on the spot. Today, she is Saint Sally.

I finally made it home by six thirty in the evening. Like a robot, I walk straight into my bedroom, strip off all of my clothes and jump in the shower. I stand there and let the hot water wash over my head. I'm absolutely exhausted. People told me this was going to be hard. People told me that you never work harder than you do when starting your own business. I had started a business before, but it was so different from this one. This one is much more difficult. There are so many moving parts, my head feels like it is going to pop off. I get out of the shower, dry myself off, and throw on a fleece and a relatively clean pair of yoga pants. I snake my way through the maze of boxes in my living room to the kitchen and pour myself a glass of wine. I ignore the unwashed dishes in the sink and the piles of unopened mail on my kitchen counter. I stand in the middle of my living room and stare at the piles of boxes everywhere. I am not sure whether to throw up, cry, or start throwing boxes out the window. I plop myself down on my sofa and swing my feet up onto a stack of boxes labeled *Candy Cups*. It hits me like a ton of bricks. I still have to make thousands and thousands of truffles. "I can't do it. I just can't do it." I glance around my apartment and I think, "I need a housekeeper."

Sunday morning, I wake up to my alarm going off at eight thirty. I had put myself to bed at around nine the night before. Eleven and a half hours of sleep and I feel like a new woman. I can do this and I am definitely getting a housekeeper. I look at my phone and I have two hundred emails, twenty-five text messages and three voicemails. Most of these are people responding to my help wanted ads. I used to get excited if I had a lot of text messages and voicemails, now I just want to pretend I lost my phone. I do however; have something to look forward to today. Ty is making me dinner at his house, he has banned me from bringing anything, and he pushed the time up so that I can make it home for my new very early bedtime. I'm due over at his place at one in the afternoon because in addition to everything else the man does for me he is helping me sort through another round of applications. I am not sure what I ever did to deserve such an amazing friend but I am grateful, so very grateful. I still haven't addressed the minor issue that I saw him with someone I am assuming is his new girlfriend. It's bothering me though. I'm going to try and broach the subject with him today.

I pack up my laptop, notebook, and a few emails I printed out from applicants that I think might be really good. I still have another one hundred or more job applicant emails to scrutinize with Ty. I begin my walk to Ty's house. He only lives about ten blocks from me; however, it seems like a different neighborhood all together. I call his side of the Back Bay the adult side. It's where I hope to live when I grow up. He lives on Marlborough Street closer to the Public Gardens. It's a quiet street lined with brownstones. Ty owns the entire building. He keeps the basement as a basement, which is rare in this part of town; most people finish off the basement level and turn it into an apartment. Ty doesn't want to deal with the hassle of a basement flooding and quite honestly doesn't think a basement apartment in the northeast is good for anyone's mental health, even on Marlborough Street. The first floor, or parlor level apartment, is occupied by a lovely widower whom Ty says came with the building. The second floor is rented out to nice young newlyweds. Ty lives on the third and fourth floors. When he bought the brownstone he gutted the upper two units and combined them into one. When you look at the brownstone from the outside it is hard to imagine how swanky and modern it is on the inside.

You enter Ty's building through two grand sets of wide wooden doors. The doors look like they are from the 1800's but of course they are now equipped with the latest security system. People can open the front door from their individual apartments while watching you on what looks like IPads mounted to their wall. The entryway has new flooring with that matches the old wood chair rail that lines the halls. The staircase is magnificent and wraps its way elegantly up the stairs. Ty's door to his apartment is new but looks old to match the hall and stairwell décor. When you enter his apartment it is like walking through a time machine. Every inch of his place is modern and sleek with all of the latest and greatest technology has to offer. It is however, warm and inviting. It has clean lines and a modern feel but the furniture and overly plush rugs are inviting. It's the kind of environment that makes you want to kick off your shoes, brew some tea, curl up with your favorite book, and never leave.

After hours of sorting through resumes while sitting on Ty's living room floor, we are done. Ty pours each of a glass of the Caymus. We toast to the fifteen new applicants I get to interview on Tuesday. The wine is smooth and scrumptious.

"You know what would go great with this?" Ty asks.

"Chocolate." I respond.

"Chocolate. When do you start production?"

"Oh, Ty, I can't even think about that yet. In about two weeks. I hope I remember how to make it." I tease.

Ty just shoots me look and grins. "Well, you had better start thinking about it. You have a $25,000.00 order to fill."

"Are you trying to give me an anxiety attack Ty? Because, it is working!"

"You can do it Lex. Teach me and I will help you."

"Ty, I can't possibly ask you to do one more thing for me. You do everything for me. Case and point, you can't even get into your second bedroom because it is filled with crap for my business."

"You can ask me to do anything for you at any time. I want you to succeed. I want you to have a storefront right down the street from my office. Honestly Lex, I am glad you have left your old line of work. Working with families of criminals, going into places where no one knows where you are. I know you said you were always safe. I understand why you did it and that the families needed the help; but, it scared me. Oh, which reminds me, I saved the Globe for you today. I figured you probably knew the story. It was this dude who was convicted of murder and now he is trying to get a book deal to tell his story."

"Well, that's not unusual. People are always trying to make money."

"Yeah, but I thought you might know the case because it happened in Los Angeles. It sounded rather horrific. Hold, let me grab the paper."

Ty heads into his office to grab the Boston Globe. I moved over to the crock-pot full of white bean chicken chili. I uncover the pot and inhale the magnificent scent. I am starving. Ty cooks, he is kind, he is amazing, and he is hot. God he is going to make someone so happy. A quick pang of jealously suddenly comes over me thinking of Ty doing this with someone else. Stop Lexi, you and Ty are friends. *You are good at friends, don't even go there.* I have to. I have to ask if that woman is his new girlfriend. I need to know if she is the one.

Ty comes back in and I quickly close the cover like a kid being caught with her hand in the cookie jar.

"Is somebody hungry?" Ty teases.

"Starving! I respond as I grab my wine glass and head to the corner of the kitchen counter as Ty lays out the article. I take one look at the picture and I feel a surge of hormones rush through my body. I feel dizzy and sick. My hands start to shake and my wine is spilling over the glass and then the glass falls and shatters on the tile floor. I nearly fall with it but Ty catches me with one arm. It was as if someone shot me with an incredible amount of adrenaline while simultaneously sucking out all of my strength.

"Lex, are you ok?"

I was listening to Ty's voice but yet felt as though I was floating over us, like I was somehow watching this happen and experiencing it at the same time.

"Oh my god" I whisper. I started to take my deep breaths. I began to focus, slowly, only on my breathing, in slowly and out slowly, in slowly and out slowly. I keep breathing and keep repeating to myself "back in the box Lexi." After a few minutes of breathing, repeating, and Ty rubbing my back, my heart rate begins to slow down below one hundred beats per minute.

"I am so sorry Ty."

"For what Lexi? I am sorry. I did not mean to upset you." Ty says in his softest most concerned voice.

"No, it's not your fault Ty. I'm sorry for my reaction, I haven't seen his face other than flashes in my head in almost three years."

"Was his family your clients?" Ty asked still concerned.

"No. No I knew him. His name is Alistair and he is the most evil, sadistic, sociopath I have ever met." I pause as I could feel rage beginning to boil from inside of me. I closed my eyes, "he is calculating, and cold. I did not like him from the minute I met him. I knew something was not right about him. I also knew who he killed." I felt myself beginning to spiral down into a very dark place. I had to stop. I straightened out my posture.

"That is all I can say right now Ty. I can't…"

Ty interrupted me, "No, Lexi. That is all you ever have to say. I am so, so sorry." Ty wrapped his arms around me and just held me. "God I am sorry." He whispered.

You are safe Lexi. Back in the box, put it back.

13

RIPPING OFF THE BAND-AID

I didn't sleep at all on Sunday night. Ty had walked me home and made sure I was safely locked in my apartment; but I was completely out of sorts after seeing the Boston Globe article. Monday was even worse. I was shaky and could not focus. I felt like I was trapped in my own skin and couldn't get out. I was basically a mess. It was all starting to get to be too much at the worst possible time. I needed all of my strength, energy and focus. I had changed my therapy appointment from Monday to Tuesday because Monday was Labor Day and Jackie was taking a long weekend.

I called Ty Monday evening and asked him to come to my therapy session with me as I needed to tell this story and I wanted him to hear it, but I only wanted to tell it once. Ty readily agreed and I sent Jackie an email to let her know and give her a heads up on how I planned on handling things. I told her I was telling this story once to the two people I needed to know it. I was going to be as matter of fact about it as I could as I feel like I am losing my mind.

I woke up Tuesday morning feeling a little angry and I think that is a good thing. I did my usual routine, skirted my way through the boxes in my living room to flip on the coffee and then back to the bathroom to jump in the shower. I throw on jeans and a nice blouse, scoop my hair up into a ponytail, and grab a cup of coffee and head downstairs to smoke a cigarette.

I sat outside sipping my coffee and taking a drag off my cigarette, a few runners went by and one coughed quite loudly while running by as if to make a statement. Now under normal circumstances, I would say that I deserved that. Smoking is a disgusting and repulsive habit. However, this morning I found myself thinking *screw you drama queen*. Yes, I was definitely angry this morning. I think that will help me. If I can just funnel the anger and focus it so that I can tell my story quickly and just get it out. I am sick and tired of this haunting me. I have stuffed this down for so long that I think with all of the stress I am under it is now starting to bubble over in bad ways. So bad that I am actually convinced that I have some creepy ghost-like person following me around Newbury Street. Since I am going to be spending the majority of my time on Newbury Street. I need to take care of this. I need to get rid of this ghost.

Ty had a seven o'clock breakfast meeting so he was meeting me in Beacon Hill. I walk up Beacon Street towards Jackie's office. I can feel my anger bubbling. This is good. I keep my mind focused on all things rational and talk myself into sticking with the details. It's the only way I can prevent my emotional mind from taking over. If I get emotional I'm not sure I will ever be able to get this story out.

I arrive at Jackie's office and Ty is sitting on the steps waiting for me. He stands up to greet me; he is looking particularly handsome in a pink button down and gray slacks. Why can't I find a man like Ty? He is so perfect and so damn hot. What man does this for a friend? What man does all of the things he does for a friend? A perfect man.

"Hi." I say.

"Hey, how are you feeling?" Ty asks as he wraps his arms around me to give me a hug.

"I'm good. Thanks for coming." I whisper.

I lead Ty up to Jackie's office. Jackie is waiting patiently for us and I introduce the two of them for the first time. It seems totally crazy to me that these two very important people in my life have never met, but they haven't. Ty and I take a seat on the couch and Jackie pulls up a chair in front of us.

"Well, I guess I need to begin. First, thank you Ty for coming. Thank you Jackie for having both of us here on such short notice." I took a deep breath. "I wanted to do this because, Jackie, you know just about everything there is to know about me, and Ty, you are my best friend and know just about everything there is to know about me as well. Except one thing that neither of you know. It is something that I tucked away in a box as best I could when I left Los Angeles. It rears its ugly head at times; and for the most part I have been able to handle it. However, now with the conversations we have been having Jackie and the incredible amount of stress in my life; things are starting to rise to the surface in negative ways. The final straw happened on Sunday at Ty's house. Ty showed me a Boston Globe article and when I saw the picture it almost brought me to my knees."

"I feel a bit to blame here."

"No." I quickly jump in. "Ty, it wasn't your fault at all. And I am sorry that happened. I am sorry I reacted that way which is why I want you to hear this."

Ty nods.

I begin. "Ok. I am just going to tell this story to get it over with. I am going to tell it, because I need to. But I am going to try to stick to the facts, so that I don't fall apart.

Ashley was my absolute best friend in Los Angeles. I have started to tell Jackie about her. I don't want to get too far into it but when you move to a city where you know no one and then you connect with someone in a way that Ashley and I did, it's life changing. We had so much fun together and just managed our way through the crazy LA life. I wouldn't have lasted a year out there without her and instead I lasted almost five. She was a wonderful, loving, insightful, hard-working, playful person. Everyone who met her just fell in love with her. She had that presence, you know, you met her and you just wanted to know her. I can't remember exactly when she met Alistair, maybe in 2010. They met in an acting class, he was new to Los Angeles and she just fell for him. He was an attorney who had opened up a small practice in Brentwood, a few miles from Beverly Hills where Ashley and I both lived. I don't know why an attorney was taking an acting class. When I asked him why he was in the class he said he was always interested in the art.

Anyway, Ashley took him under her wing and she did everything she could to help him. I met him about two months later. I was really looking forward to it, as she was so enthralled with him. I saw him and almost immediately I didn't like him. He made the hair on the back of my neck stand up. He was tall and handsome and charming and full of shit. He said he was gay but I don't think he was. I think it was all an act, I don't know why, but he was lying. Maybe that is why he was taking the acting classes, to be a better liar.

The three of us spent a great deal of time together much to my dismay. He always seemed to be showing up or weaseling his way into our plans. I actually had to check myself on it once to be sure that I wasn't just jealous. I wasn't. I just didn't like him. He gave me the creeps. He had this weird habit. He would always be looking at you out of the corner of his eye. When you looked at him he would quickly flit his eye back straight ahead. He always did that; it was so bizarre.

One week I was out of town working with clients. I had texted Ashley a couple of times and she never responded. A day went by and I tried calling. She never answered. After two days I was flying home and I texted again from the airport before my plane took off to no avail. It was really unusual for her to go four hours without texting me but this was now about four days so I was really concerned. I landed at LAX and turned on my phone and I had three text messages from Ashley. They all said basically the same thing: asking where I was; that she was really sick and would I please come over. I tried calling but she did not pick up. I texted her back saying I was at the airport and that I would be there in about thirty minutes, asking what was wrong and what she needed. She simply replied she was really sick, please come right over." I took a break from speaking and a couple of deep breaths. I looked around at Ty and Jackie before I continued.

"Something just wasn't sitting right with me. I can't explain it but it wasn't'. While I waited for my bag at the baggage claim I called a good friend of mine from the Beverly Hills Police Department and explained the situation. He said he would send some people over to her place and do a wellness check. I got my bags, jumped in a cab and had the cab driver head straight to Ashley's place. The cab I was in was heading down Olympic Boulevard towards Doheny, Ashley's street. Doheny was blocked off with Police cars. Now mind you, we lived in a very nice, safe neighborhood. People can say what they want about LA, but Beverly Hills was very tame. To see police cars blocking off Doheny at Olympic meant something very bad. Ashley lived a block and a half up from Olympic on Doheny between Gregory and Charleville. My hope was the something bad was not her because the road was blocked at Olympic. I was wrong." I pause, remembering the shear pain of it all.

"Alistair kidnapped and held Ashley in her apartment for days. He had tied her up and beat her up. He killed her by strangling her to death. When the police arrived he had already killed her. They estimated she had died hours prior to their arrival. Alistair held the police at bay with a gun. The standoff went on for hours and somehow they eventually got him out." I stop. My head is still hanging down as I stare at the floor. I focused on one spot throughout the whole story. It was the only way to get it out without crying.

Ty reaches over and grabs my hand. "I am so sorry Lexi."

"How are you feeling Lex?" Jackie asks.

"Numb." I respond.

"May I ask some questions Lex?" Ty asks as he squeezes my hand.

His squeeze triggers me to finally take my eyes off the carpet and look up at him. I straighten my body from its slouching position. "Of course."

"If I am understanding all of this correctly, it sounds as if he wanted to kill you too?"

I take a quick breath. "Yeah."

Ty clears his throat. "Why?"

I look over at Jackie, raise my eyebrows and shake my head. There is that question again. Why? The one that when left unanswered, can slowly eat away at your core. "That is unclear. It was a very violent event. He has a lot of hatred. He spoke to authorities and then suddenly stopped talking. From what I understand, he was, or had become Ashley's attorney. I don't know. Ashley had a trust fund. That is what made Ashley even more amazing. She didn't have to work; but she did, at a coffee shop. She didn't need to serve people every day to pay her bills, but she loved people. She wanted to be around people. Ashley grew up an only child with a single mother. However, her father, who died suddenly when she was young, was very wealthy. Her mother managed the money very well. When she died she left Ashley with a nice trust. It was not one where she could live some extravagant lifestyle, but enough to pay her bills. I never knew she began to use Alistair as her attorney. She never mentioned any of it to me and we talked about everything.

Alistair was calculating. He picked Ashley and he hurt her. He was violent. He may have just killed her because he is sick. He may have killed her to try and get her money. I don't know. He's evil, that I can tell you." I stop because I could feel the horrible, violent emotions beginning to churn in the pit of my stomach.

"But why you Lexi, why did he want to kill you?" Ty asks.

"I don't know. He stopped talking to the police. He was the one texting me. He was the one using Ashley's phone to get me to her place. Maybe he thought I knew things, that I could pin him in an investigation? I have no idea."

Ty cleared his throat again and I looked over at him. His eyes were filled with water. "Are you ok Ty? I am sorry."

"Yes. I have to go. I have an investor meeting I absolutely have to be at. I will call you later Lexi. Thank you." He kissed me on the forehead. He stood up and shook Jackie's hand and then left.

"Shit." I said.

"It's ok Lexi. It was a lot to take in and he needs to handle it how he needs to handle it." Jackie tried to reassure me.

"It's not ok Jackie. It's friggin' crazy. I should have done it with more time. I don't want to freak him out."

"Lexi, Ty is a grown man. He will be fine. It is you I am worried about. This happened to you. And what article in the Boston Globe made you break down?" Jackie asked.

"Well, apparently, Alistair is trying to get a book deal or something. I didn't read the article. I couldn't."

"Oh, Lexi." Jackie says. "Shall I pull up the article?"

"Yeah, look to see if there is anything in the LA Times."

Jackie does just that and discovers that although Alistair is seeking a book deal, he has not had any takers. "No one seems to want to help him tell his story." Jackie reports.

"What story?"

Jackie looks back to her computer screen and looks up at me. "He wants to tell his side, why he did it."

"That sick bastard."

"And it also clearly says that he is going to be in prison for as long as he lives."

At that point I break down. I'm not sure why. Maybe because I told the story, maybe I had a big sense of relief that others realize he is evil. Maybe I was always worried in the back of my head that he would get out, or somehow manipulate someone.

"What are you feeling?" Jackie asks.

"I bit of relief and a lot of guilt. I have beaten myself up for years with the 'why' questions. Why didn't I contact the police sooner? Why didn't I stop her from seeing him? Why didn't I try harder to let her know how evil he was?"

"How could you have known this Lexi? This was unpredictable."

"Was it? The signs were there Jackie. He started to come between us. He started to demand more of her time alone. We would still speak all of the time; but there was less time spent together because he demanded her time. I started to hear her say things like, 'I can't disappoint Alistair' or 'he would be very upset if,'. Ashley's personality began to change a bit. She became less magnetic and more of a shrinking violet. She was afraid of him."

"Lexi, I understand what you are saying but that behavior, his manipulative behavior would not indicate to anyone this level of violence. I mean were there any signs of physical abuse?"

"No. But all of the other classic emotional abuse signs were loud and clear. She was living in fear. Her life began to revolve around making him happy, this self-reported gay friend. And he changed. I saw that. He went from worshiping every word that came out of her mouth to berating her for the 'stupid things' she would say. I stepped in once and said something to him. I stood up to him."

"What happened?"

"He shot me a look, a stone-cold death stare. It scared me. After that, he began to really cut into the time Ashley and I would spend together." I paused and stared blankly at the floor. "And there you have it, my guilt. I knew something was very wrong. I didn't do enough to get her away from him."

"You did try Lexi."

"I did. I absolutely did try to speak with her. I tried to get in between them. I failed."

"Lexi, isn't losing your best friend painful enough or do you need to walk around with this guilt too?"

My eyes opened wide and I look at Jackie.

"What purpose does this guilt serve?"

"I don't know."

"What are you scared of?" Jackie asks.

She asked the right question. She wasn't going to let me hide behind the things I have no control over. She got right to the core. I am scared. "I feel like I..." I pause looking for the right words. "I feel like, I am not sure exactly how to say this, but I feel as though I cheated death somehow. You know, like, the accident that happens right in front of you or right behind you. Somehow, you missed it. But it could've been you. You should be dead too. I feel scared and anxious a lot. I feel like how many times can I do that before it catches me."

"You mean because you survived the car accident as well?" Jackie clarifies.

"Yes."

"Is that all you are scared of?"

I want to say yes; Jackie is not letting me off easy. "No. I mean, yes that is big. I do feel as though I am always looking over my shoulder. I am anxious and more suspicious of everyone. But, I'm also very scared about everyone else in my life. This is going to sound completely crazy Jackie. I don't want them to get hurt because of me. Hanging on to my guilt, reminds me of this." I could barely squeak the sentence out before I just completely broke down in tears. That is what scares me the most; one more person in my life getting hurt.

"None of this is your fault Lexi. And you can't let it prevent you from loving the people who clearly love you." Jackie says in her calmest voice.

I nod. "I know, I know. But there is that irrational part of my mind that thinks I survive, but the ones I love…" the tears overwhelm me. I can't say it. I just cry silently and think *the ones I love die, they die.*

Jackie did her best over the next thirty minutes to put me back together. I had to pull it together as I am interviewing fifteen people beginning at one in the afternoon.

I left Jackie's office feeling as though I had been hit by a mack truck and then it went into reverse and ran me over again. I'm feeling so guilty for brining Ty to my session. That was such a dumb decision on my part. I traumatized him for no reason. He didn't need to hear that story. What the fuck was I thinking? I wanted him to know that I have reasons for being the way I am. I wanted him to see that if he was with me, that he was putting his life at risk. Why did I do that to my best friend? I have lived with this story for years. He is just hearing it. I tell it like I am reading a script. I am numb. I can't imagine how he is feeling. God, I am an idiot! I pull out my phone and send Ty a text reading: *Hey, are you ok? I am so sorry I had you come.*

I decide to stroll down by the Charles. I have some time before my first interview and I need to clear my head. Being by the water has always had a calming effect on me. I'm really hoping it works extra well today. All these thoughts are just running through my head.

It's weird. My parents died in a freak car accident when I was five years old. I survived. It wasn't anyone's fault. A crazy thunderstorm rolled through as we were driving home. I remember hearing the lightning bolt strike as if it was hitting the car. I was in the backseat and it frightened me so much that I drew my legs up to my chest. Apparently that move, pulling my legs up to my chest, is why I can still walk today and maybe even the reason I survived. The next thing I remember is waking up to a man pulling me out of the car and I was screaming for my parents. The lightning bolt hit a tree and it crashed on top of the car killing both of my parents in the front seat. I pulled my legs up just in time or I would have lost my legs. *I survive, the people I love die.*

When you're a child and you lose your parents like I did, it is a weird thing. People feel badly for you. They never really know what to say to you so instead they tend to whisper. I used to want to scream, "I'm right here. I know what you're whispering about. Stop whispering!" No one ever talked to me about it. They would just give me the sad face and ask how I was doing. The only people I could talk to were my grandparents and my therapist. It was hard not to speak openly about my parents. I was often told not to because other people didn't know how to handle it or what to say. So instead of being able to talk about how great my parents were it became more like a secret, something I too, could only whisper about.

When I was young, I didn't really experience survivor guilt. Instead I made up a story in my head that my parents were the super heroes who lost their lives for me. I used to hear adults talk about that stuff all of the time. I would hear people say things like, "I would lose my right arm for my child," or "I would throw myself in front of a train for my child." How I thought of it was that my parents were the heroic ones who actually did make the ultimate sacrifice for me. Now, where I got tripped up as an adolescent and young adult was what could I possibly do in life to honor their sacrifice. I put a lot of pressure on myself. It took a lot of therapy to move beyond my over-achieving, nothing is ever-good enough state of mind. I'm not sure I ever got over it, but I manage it better.

That was the beautiful thing about Ashley. She really helped me realize what I was doing was amazing and that I was allowed to enjoy life too. And then Ashley was murdered. *I survive and the people I love die.*

When I think of Ashley, my emotions cycle very quickly between sadness and anger. Like right now, I am so sad. I wish I could call her and ask for her guidance. I wish she could be here to experience this process with me. She loved my chocolate. She actually outlined the first business plan for my shop. Of course back then we thought I would do it in Beverly Hills and it would be the chocolate shop to the stars. The lump in my throat forms and my eyes begin to fill with tears. I miss her so much. *Fuck you Alistair. Fuck you.*

I pull out my phone to see if I have any messages from Ty. Not a one. I send him another text of a sad face. God why did I have him come? I am such an idiot. I can't lose Ty. I love him. Is my subconscious fear so strong that I actually sabotaged the best thing in my life?

14

RADIO SILENCE AND A KISS

After what turned into two days of interviewing, I managed to hire two more people. I think that is all I need to get started. I am hoping as the shop opens and I get into the swing of things I will have people dropping by and looking for work. Eventually I am going to need more help. For now, however, I am sending the entire crew through the food safety course and hoping we can make it work without exhausting everyone.

My moods continue to swing between sadness and anger. Although, admittedly it is mostly anger. It is now Friday and I haven't heard from Ty since Tuesday, this makes me sad. I try my best not to bombard him with phone calls or text messages, but I do. I know he needs time to process things and he also happens to be a very busy man. However, I feel as though I caused this and to be responsible for shutting down one of the most important people in my life is a horrible feeling. This is when I start to get angry. I'm frustrated by the fact that Alistair is continuing to cause pain in my life. I realize that it's me who is giving this evil person power in my life. Alistair is hopefully rotting in a prison on the other side of the country, yet he occupies my thoughts and is affecting my relationships with people he has never known. This is the power I am giving him and I need to change that. That of course is much easier said than done. I know it will be something I have to work on constantly in therapy. This week, when I feel the anger begin to swirl in my gut, I try and focus the energy to my work. I am starting my dream and I am not going to give anyone the power to ruin it. As quickly as I become that power-ful, I have to suck back the tears that begin to form when I look at my phone and see nothing from Ty. When the hell did my phone get so powerful in my life? Shit.

It is now ten in the morning and I need to get back to my store-front. It looks fabulous. It's amazing to me how much work the guys have gotten done in such a short amount of time. This morning I have a present being delivered. I am getting my chocolate Enrober. It was a big investment but one I'm hoping pays off quickly as far as the chocolate production is concerned. Throughout my truffle making career I have always been hand-dipping my chocolates. This works fine when making four hundred truffles a day. However, now that the production is going to have to go up to somewhere between two and five thousand per day, I need the Enrober. The Enrober is the cool machine that you have may seen on television. It's the machine that tempers the chocolate and coats each individual truffle. When hand-dipping the chocolate I could produce about one hundred per hour. This machine will bump that number up to closer to one thou-sand per hour. It is a significant investment but one that will not only give me substantial returns but also saves my body. Tempering the chocolate by hand can take quite a toll on your shoulders and arms from all of the stirring. I could not imagine doing that all day every day. My shoulder would be shot in less than a month.

I turn onto Newbury Street from Mass Ave and I am definitely moving at a quick pace. I think I might be just a little excited to get my new chocolate coating machine. I cross over Newbury Street to run into Starbucks, yes, my diet is almost one hundred per cent caffeine these days. Just as I open the door to walk into Starbucks, Patrick is walking out hand in hand with a pretty, petite brunette. Patrick sees me and quickly becomes flustered and releases the bru-nette's hand.

"Lexi, um hi."

"Hi Patrick." I reply sounding not really interested as I continue my forward motion. I am on a mission.

"Lexi, um, this is my wife Karen." Patrick says still flustered.

"Hi Karen, nice to meet you. I'm sorry I'm in a rush."

Nice to meet you." Karen says rather coldly, not that I blame her. Karen is a rather plain looking woman but pretty. She isn't tall maybe five foot three and has short dark hair. Actually her hair cut looks quite similar to Patrick's. She looks young. She doesn't have any wrinkles. She has a very proper appearance wearing a navy blue wrap dress, simple blue ballet flats, and a string of white pearls around her neck.

"How is it that you two know each other?" Karen asks while looking up at her husband.

Patrick jumps in nervously. "Lexi is a friend of John's."

"Oh." Is all Karen says as she looks at me with pursed lips.

"How is your shop coming along?" Patrick asks and then turns to his wife to tell her that I am opening a chocolate shop. Just like that his wife now has interest in me.

"Oh, wow, here?" Karen asks.

"Yes, just up the street. And again, I am really sorry, but I am just getting some coffee and then have to race up there for a delivery. It was really nice meeting you Karen. Great to see you Patrick." I reach into my purse and hand Karen a "coming soon" card that has just enough information to get people excited, talking, and hopefully check out my website. I don't even wait for a response and just run inside. I may have been a bit rude to just hand her my information and flee, but I have to be a shameless self- promoter. I have things to do and Patrick is an odd duck I don't want to spend any time with.

By four-thirty in the afternoon I felt as though it was midnight. It took two hours to get my Enrober installed and working. It then took another four hours for the guy to test it and train me. I now think I will be able to run the machine on my own without ruining it or worse harming myself.

The guys have all packed up and left for the night. I think it is about time I do the same. I check my phone and I have three text messages unfortunately none of them were from Ty. They were all from Patrick. The first read: *Hi Lexi, great to see you today.* The second read: *I want to apologize if it was at all uncomfortable running into me with my wife.* And the last and craziest read: *I am sorry to say this via text but my wife and I are back together. She wants me to not communicate with you ever again. I am sorry about all of this Lexi.*

This guy is delusional. I don't even know what to think or how to feel. He is sort of scary crazy. I want to scream into my phone "I don't give a shit!!!" I don't. And I do not even text him back. I do not want to add any fuel to his delusional fire. I need a shower.

I grab my things and lock up my storefront. I head up Newbury Street to Deluca's Market to grab a sandwich and some chips, otherwise known as my dinner. I walk out of Deluca's Market dinner in hand and I look across the street. The singing homeless guy is sitting across the street singing away. I stand there for a second, pondering whether I should go across the street and try and talk to him. I don't know why I was pondering this; the guy never talks to anyone. I am really tired. As I begin to turn to my right to saunter down Newbury Street, I hear him: "Casper the friendly ghost, the friendliest ghost you know. Left, Left, Left, right, left." The homeless guy sings. This guy is totally screwing with me. But then, I did turn to my left and I saw him: the strange, creepy guy. I just caught a glimpse of him as he turned to head down Fairfield Street, but I'm certain it was him. He was wearing the same baseball hat. I turned and started running after him.

I zigged and zagged my way through the Friday night crowds saying lots of "pardon me's and sorry's." I quickly turned onto Fairfield and I couldn't see my ghost. I ran to the alley and looked down to the left to see nothing. I looked across Fairfield, down the alley to the right and I could see him, his back to me walking briskly down the alley. I quickly sprinted across Fairfield narrowly missing being hit by a biker. A ranger rover was pulling out of the alley and I looked at the driver it wasn't my ghost. I ran passed the Range Rover and looked down the Alley. My ghost was gone.

What the hell am I doing? I am chasing some unknown person down an alley because some homeless guy signaled me through his song that my ghost was present. And what the hell was I going to do if I actually caught up with the guy? What was my plan? Confront the guy by myself in an alley? And what exactly has he done wrong except seem a bit creepy? Which is totally subjective opinion. I stand in the alley and those were my thoughts. This is ridiculous. I need to get home, take a shower, and get some serious sleep.

I walk back up the alley and turn on to Fairfield Street and run smack into Patrick.

"Lexi."

"Oh, sorry Patrick, I wasn't paying attention." I say while thinking to myself what the hell are you doing here?

"No, problem, it was me, I was daydreaming. I'm glad I ran into you though. I sent you some text messages. Did you get them?" Patrick asks in an overly concerned fashion.

"Yes." I have no words and no time for this.

"I'm so sorry Lexi. God, I feel like such a jerk. I never meant to hurt you."

"You didn't hurt me Patrick. Good luck." I say as I try to skirt around him.

"Lexi, please don't be mad." Patrick says as he takes a step to the side and gets in my way. That is it. I can't take it.

"Patrick, I'm not mad. I don't care. I don't like you and I never did. Please just leave me alone and focus on your marriage." This time I took a quick step to the left and ran across the street. This guy is a lunatic.

I get down to Commonwealth Ave and start walking towards Beacon Street constantly checking over my shoulder to be certain Patrick or my creepy ghost is not following me. Now that I think about it, Patrick is creepier than my ghost. What the heck does his wife see in him? Not only is he creepy, he's out of his mind, and quite frankly if he's pulling this with me then he is being a real jerk to his wife. Whatever, their relationship is the last thing I need to be concerned about. I should be concerned about the weird man who keeps showing up on Newbury Street. Who is he and what does he want? Maybe he is just a guy who is creepy and happens to be in the neighborhood when I am. Except, he keeps disappearing as quickly as he shows up, that is unsettling. I need to tell someone. Of course the one person I would like to tell is not speaking to me.

I get home and head right for the shower. After a long hot shower, I am feeling nothing but less dirty. I stand in front of my bed wearing my yoga pants and a tee shirt and strongly consider just crawling in even though it is only six thirty in the evening. This is the hard part of being single. I'm freaked out, stressed out and exhausted. This is when I could use a partner, someone to talk to, and someone to help me sort through everything and tell me it's going to be all right. My friends are terrific and they listen as best and as often as they can. But it's Friday evening; they're all out running after their kids. Living life, the way it should be, or at least how I've always been told it should be. I don't know if I could handle any of their lives but it would be nice to have a partner in crime. When you're single, you are it. You are the only one. If you're stressed you deal with it, if you don't have enough money it is up to you to make more, if you have a medical issue you deal with the fear by yourself, if you are too busy to shop or do laundry or clean then those things don't get done. And if you are sad or scared you console yourself. Yes, a partner would be nice. Then again, I survive and the people I love die. Losing one more person that I love might actually do me in for good.

I grab water from my kitchen, walk over to my couch, lie down and turn on the television. The TV is helpful in making these nights a little less lonely. If I am so wonderful, how come I am always alone? I try not to dwell or focus too much on the lonely feelings I have. However, sometimes they win. Sometimes reality just stares you down and wears you down and you feel really sad. There are moments when being alone hurts so much and there is nothing to take that pain away. All you can do is get through it. I keep telling myself not to cry. I just need to get through it. I need Ty. *Please universe, don't let me lose him.*

I woke suddenly to what I thought was someone calling my name. I sit up and the TV is still on. I feel asleep on the couch. I swore someone called my name. Maybe I was dreaming. I walk over to my front door and look out the peephole. I don't see anyone. And I especially don't see Ty. I open the door and look down the hall. No one is there. My wish is now completely unfulfilled. I check my phone, nothing from Ty. I decide to crawl into bed and hope the morning will bring some relief.

"Lexi!" My name was being yelled so loudly it felt like it was coming from my living room.

"Lexi!" I hear it again. I look out my bedroom window onto Beacon Street. I can't believe my eyes. Across the street is Patrick, standing, well, not really standing more like swaying. This can't be happening. Patrick is looking rather intoxicated, standing across the street, yelling my name. Now the man has crossed a line. Without turning on any lights, I get out of bedroom and grab my phone. It is ten thirty at night; the night building manager doesn't leave until eleven so Patrick can't just walk into the building undetected. Do I call the police? I don't want to create a scene, but this guy is unpredictable. Just as I am about to dial 911 I hear a faint knock. I gasp. The door is still bolted shut. A fear came over me and I can't move. I hear the knock again and "Lexi?"

I quickly look out the peephole. *Thank you universe.* I unbolt the door, "Ty!"

Ty walks in and I begin to speak. Ty holds up his hand to stop me while shaking his head no. He backs me up against the wall, he is not speaking, and he is just staring at me. He puts his hand on the side of my face and kisses me. I feel my knees weakening.

"Where did you go?" I whisper.

Ty pulls back and looks at me with intensity. "I needed time. I was angry. I know everything about you but not this." Ty stops and gently grabs my lips with his then releases them. "That anger didn't last long. I then felt a different anger, more like rage. I was incensed by the thought of someone wanting to hurt you and me not being there to protect you. Then I got sad, when I thought of what if something different had happened and I didn't have you right here, right now, every Sunday." Ty paused, and looked deep into my eyes as he caressed my cheek, still holding me against the wall, still inches from my face. "Then I got mad at you, for getting in my head with all of your stupid rules about relationships and dating. I calmed down when I realized that this was your way of protecting yourself. I know how scared you are and I know why. After feeling and considering all of these things I decided she's worth it. She is worth all of the potential pain and heartache. I can't go one more day pretending that I am not in love with every crazy, neurotic, over analyzing, over achieving, smart, sexy, powerful, sweet and beautiful ounce of you. And you and your little anxious, scared, rabbit feet are going to have to stay right here and deal with the fact that I love you."

I inhaled quickly upon hearing those words.

Ty places his other hand on the other side of my face and pulls me into him. His kiss is so passionate so fueled by emotion it is overwhelming me. My body is becoming weak. I kiss him as tears run down my cheeks. His hand slides down my back, gently over my ass and then scoops me up onto him. I wrap my legs around his waist and our lips never part. Both of his arms wrapped tightly around my waist as he carries me into the bedroom. Ty gently lays me down on the bed and is on top of me.

"Ty," I whisper.

Ty looks at me. The streetlights shining into my bedroom window allow me to see his face and eyes. He looks at me with pure longing. His eyes are soft. He straddles me on his knees and sits up. He removes his shirt. All I see is his dark skin and muscles bumping from his abdomen. He leans down and hovers over me, his shoulders are strong and cut. I run my hands down along his arms feeling every protruding muscle. He kisses me again and the fire inside of me erupts. We had sex like two lovers who had not seen each other in months. Later, we made love. I made love to Ty.

My alarm went off at five thirty in the morning. I awoke the same way I fell asleep, naked and wrapped up in Ty's arms. I slid over and silenced my alarm. I made a move to slowly slide out of bed but Ty pulled me closer and tightened his arms around me.

"Stay."

"I have to get the coffee for the guys."

Ty groaned and rolled over. He fished through his pants and pulled out his phone. He sent a text message to someone, put his phone down and rolled back over to me. "There, you're all set."

"Ty, what did you do?" I asked.

"I texted your crew that you were tied up but that we would be there with lunch for them so they needed to send me their lunch request."

I giggled, "thank you."

Ty wrapped his arms around me and kissed my neck. "Go back to sleep Lexi, you need it."

Apparently I did need it. I fell back asleep and woke up to my coffee maker beeping. I don't remember making coffee. Ty is not in bed with me. I look up at my clock and it is ten in the morning. Shit. I fly out of bed, run into the bathroom and jump into the shower. Ten in the morning I am so late. I have no idea where Ty is and oh my god, I slept with Ty. I don't even have time to deal with or wrap my head around the emotional ramifications of my actions. My mind is already racing at warp speed going through my list of everything I need to get done. I get out of the shower and squeeze the excess water out of my hair. I get dressed and head into my living room just as Ty is opening my apartment door.

"You're awake?" Ty smiles brightly as he puts down a brown bag on the kitchen counter.

"I am." I respond. I don't move because I am not exactly sure what to do here.

Thankfully Ty does. He comes over to me and wraps his arms around me and gives me a squeeze. "I made coffee and brought breakfast."

I relax for a second in Ty's embrace. "Thank you. Unfortunately, I have to take everything to go. I have the appliance guys coming. I think they may already be there…"

Ty interrupts my rant by putting both of his hands up in the air as he moves over to the coffee maker. "It is all set; you don't have to be anywhere except right here."

"What do you mean?"

"I went down to your storefront this morning. I met with the guys, brought them coffee. The appliances were delivered while I was there; they are all being installed as we speak. They have my cell phone number in case they need anything. I ordered and paid for everyone's lunch, which is being delivered at noon."

I look at Ty in shock. "Seriously?"

"Seriously." Ty responds with a wink.

My eyes begin to well up. It may not seem like much but what Ty did for me was amazing. He just jumped in and took care of things for me without me even asking. He let me sleep. He did all of my minor tasks that seem to take up a lot of my time. He did all of this so that I could get much needed sleep and eat breakfast sitting down. I moved over to the couch and plopped down. And then I started to cry. I don't know why I was crying but I was. I guess I just realized how amazing it is to have some help and how much I love him.

"Baby girl." Ty says as he comes over to the couch with coffee in hand. "Why are you crying?"

I inhale deeply, "I don't know."

Ty laughs and gets up to grab me some tissues. He returns with not only tissues, but also a plate full of fruit, bagels, butter, and cheese. Looking at the amazing plate of food, I suddenly realize how hungry I am. "Thank you Ty!"

"You okay?"

"Yes." I say sniffling and wiping my tears.

"Good, let's eat. I'm starving." Ty says as he picks up a bagel.

"So last night had the craziest dream." I begin as I layer cheese on top of a half a of a bagel. "You came over to my apartment and we had sex." I wanted to say made love, but I couldn't bring myself to say the L word.

"Really, sounds hot, how was it?" Ty asks in a rather nonchalant tone.

I finish chewing, "It was good."

Ty drops his bagel on the plate. "It was good." He pauses. "Good?" He takes the coffee mug and bagel out of my hands and places them on the table. He reaches around my waist and pulls me up on top of him so I am straddling his waist. He reaches his hands up and gently pulls my face towards his and kisses me. I am melting again. In one swift move he stands up while holding me against him, walks into my bedroom, and lays me down on the bed. Still hovering over me, his lips inches from mine he says, "Clearly I have some work to do."

Thank you Universe, it wasn't just a dream.

15

THE TALK

Ty and I separated for the afternoon. We both decided it was the only way either of us would get any work done. We also decided that we would meet for dinner in a neutral location, meaning a restaurant, at eight in the evening. We both know we need to have a real conversation about what is going on with us and it clearly can't happen at either of our places as we seem to be like dogs in heat.

It took every ounce of will power I had to focus on my list of tasks for the day. Thankfully most of the tasks, although painfully tedious, did not require a lot of brainpower. When you begin a business you realize what you can't do. This lesson is usually expensive and wastes a great deal of your precious time. For example, trying to create your own marketing materials, invitations, logos, or website. Things a graphic artist can do for you in about one eighth of the time with a much more polished look. You also learn that you have to try to do everything you can to save money. I remind myself of this as I sit on my living room floor labeling all of my soft opening invitations.

This is the perfect task for me to be doing as I try to come to grips with all that has been happened over the last sixteen hours. I had sex with Ty, a lot. I want to call my girlfriends and discuss every last detail, but I can't. Ty and I still haven't had a conversation about what happened and where we are going, or worse, not going. I can't get my friends all excited and roped into my drama when I am not even sure which end is up, or worse, down. He said he loved me but who was that woman? There are so many different ways I could freak out about this situation right now, I have to stay out of my head and focus on my current task: *invitation in envelope, label, stamp, seal, next.*

By seven thirty in the evening I am dressed and ready to go. My living room is now not only covered in boxes but also stacks of invitations waiting patiently to be mailed. I look around my apartment and shake my head at the mess. It will all have to wait, this, Ty, is a much bigger priority. I do one last check in my bathroom mirror. I almost don't recognize myself. I actually took the time to do my hair and apply makeup. I check my outfit; it is cute but doesn't scream high maintenance. Of course Ty knows I am not high maintenance. He knows me as well as any of my friends. I am fretting over my appearance. I'm nervous. Oh no, I'm nervous to meet Ty. I also have, at the pit of my stomach, something I am not sure how to talk about. The beautiful woman whom I saw Ty with outside of Sonsie, who is she? I cringe when I think of his hand being placed on the small of her back.

This is crazy; this is exactly what I do not want. I don't want nerves, anxiety, jealousy, or any of the bad crap that goes along with a relationship. I just want my best friend and that carefree relationship with sex added, and the partnership piece, and all of the good stuff that goes along with a relationship. *Stop thinking Lexi; you are so much better when you don't think. For the sake of everyone involved, stop thinking.*

I feel the quickening of my heart rate as I ride the elevator down to the lobby of my building. Ty and I decided to meet at the restaurant so that we would not risk forgoing food and conversation for sex. I walk out the doors of my building and Ty is standing on the sidewalk.

"Hi," I say poorly hiding my confusion as I walk up the steps to the sidewalk.

"You look amazing." Ty responds as he leans in and kisses me. "You didn't think I was going to let you walk to the restaurant alone did you?" Ty asks.

"I did. And I wasn't offended by it. I thought it was our restraint guarantee."

"Hmm. Well, what kind of gentleman would I be if I didn't pick up my date or was unable to show restraint?" Ty asks as he grabs my hand and we start walking towards Mass Ave.

I shake my head. "Ty I don't know how to respond. I'm not sure if I should be good on-a-date Lexi, or sarcastic Lexi, or the Lexi I am when I am with my best friend."

Ty laughs, "just be you."

"Ty, I will totally screw that up."

"That is the beautiful thing Lexi, you can't. I know you. I know the over-achieving type A Lexi, I know the sarcastic Lexi, I know the sensitive bleeding-heart Lexi, and I even know the Lexi who breaks. You can't screw up being you, not with me anyway."

"Are you trying to get in my pants?" I ask reaching for sarcasm to avoid crying.

Ty laughs, "See, you can't screw up being you."

We reach the restaurant. Ty selected Abe and Louie's, a perfect choice. It is fun, always packed with people, and the food is outstanding. The hostess leads us through the restaurant to a private room. The room consists of one table set for two. The table is tastefully decorated with candles and a small round vase of multicolored roses. Ty pulls out my chair as I sit. The hostess hands us our menus. The first waiter comes in quickly to fill our water glasses and places a decadent looking basket of bread on the table. A second waiter is right behind him with a bottle of wine. He introduces himself and shows the wine to Ty who nods approvingly. He opens the bottle and pours for Ty to taste.

"Perfect." Ty says to the waiter and then looks at me, "you are going to love this."

The waiter pours my glass with wine and then Ty's. Ty asks the waiter to give us some time with the menus. I'm so nervous my hands are shaking; I don't dare pick up the glass for fear of spilling wine everywhere. I am with Ty, my best friend. What is going on with me?

"Lexi," Ty begins, "I'm suddenly so nervous I don't know if I can pick up my glass of wine. And I'm not sure why, I mean, this is you."

I laugh and tear up all at the same time. Of course, Ty says exactly what I am feeling and exactly what I need him to say. Of course he does. "Ty, I'm shaking so badly, I would spill wine everywhere."

Ty smiles. "I need help starting this conversation."

My heart sinks; maybe this is a conversation I don't want to have. What if Ty doesn't want to be with me? What if he just said those things in the heat of the moment? What if he wants things to go back to the way things were before last night? Maybe things should go back to the way they were? My head is spinning. *People I love die and I survive.*

"Lexi?" Ty asks.

"I'm scared." Is all I can manage to say.

"Me too." Ty says as he reaches across the table for my hand.

I stare at his hand wrapped around mine. I love his hands. I love his touch. I love watching his thumb gently rub mine. "I guess I am wondering what happened. I get why you needed space after that crazy story. But, I..."

Ty interrupts me before I can finish. "Lex," he begins in a much stronger voice, "I did need some time. I admit my initial reaction was anger. My immature side took over as I said last night. I was hurt that I knew every detail about you except that story."

I try to speak to defend myself and Ty just holds up his hand signaling he was not done.

"I meant what I said last night Lex. I love you, and I have for a long time."

Suddenly, I feel anger in the pit of my stomach. "Then who was she?" Shit I can't believe those words just came out of my mouth.

Ty leans back with a confused look on his face. "Who was who?"

I inhale quickly, too late to back track now, my train of sabotage has left the station. "A few weeks ago I saw you walking into Sonsie with her. She was tall and gorgeous. And I could see the chemistry between the two of you."

"Hmm." Ty gives me a half smile. "Did you get a good look at her?"

What kind of question is that? "Yes, good enough to see how pretty she was and to see the way you smiled at her."

"Are you sure?"

"Yes Ty." I am getting defensive.

"Lex, that was Colette."

"Collette?" I can't hide my shock. "But I thought she was in Paris?"

"She was, is. She came over to the States for some meetings in her New York office and stopped in Boston for lunch with me on her way back to Paris."

"Oh." I am deflated and beyond embarrassed by my behavior.

"Look Lexi, you can be jealous of women but not my sister."

"I'm sorry I'm an ass." I put my face in my hands.

"Lexi, hear me, please. I love you."

The lump in my throat feels big and hard. The tears streaming down my face are certain to be the color of my black mascara. Every single person on the planet should feel this loved, at least once. It is the most amazing feeling; yet, I'm so wrought with angst and fear I can't speak or move. My eyes drop to the table. *The people I love die and I survive.* I would not survive losing him. "I'm so scared I will fuck this up." I say without raising my eyes.

Ty reaches over and gently lifts up my chin. I force myself to look at him. "That is not what you're afraid of Lexi. Yes, someday I will die. But not before experiencing my life with you, all in."

I half stood up out of my chair, reached my hands across the table for Ty's face and kissed him. Ty stood up and pulled me out from behind the table. He wrapped his arms around me and kissed me in a way that made my body feel as though warm liquid was running through it. He stopped kissing me, pulled out $400.00 from his wallet, threw it on the table, and led me out the door.

16

SEVENTEEN DAYS AND A WAKE UP

As the grand opening of Truffle This comes closer my life is defined by the countdown to the big day. When I worked in the prison system the inmates used to define the time left until their release in terms of days and a wake up. So if it was Monday, and they were being released on Friday, they would have 3 days and a wake up. The day you were in did not count and your release day was considered a "wake up". I thoroughly loved the work I did in the prison system; hence I adopted their terminology. Today is Tuesday, September 15, 2015; I have seventeen days and a wake up. Shit.

My alarm starts beeping at 5:00 in the morning. I hit snooze four times, my neighbors must love me at this point. It's nearly fall now and the mornings have a chill to them that makes you just want to curl under your covers and SLEEP. I'm seriously becoming sleep deprived. For the few weeks, except for a few occasions when Ty steps in and insists I curl up with him, I have been going to bed around midnight and getting up at 5:00 a.m. Five hours of sleep a night is one thing in your 20's, it is a whole different story in your late 30's. I know something has got to give, it just can't be me!

I sit up in bed and ponder if one more hour of sleep would help me or hurt me. It's Tuesday. "No, I think to myself, can't do it". The construction crew is starting at 6:30 which means I have to be at the shop by 6:15, with coffee, I will myself to get up.

I swing my legs out from under the covers and rest my head on my knees. I fell asleep. My alarm goes off yet again. I have learned not to actually turn off my alarm until I am physically standing by my bed, it seems as though I can fall asleep anywhere these days. I stand up; shut my alarm off and head to the kitchen to make my coffee. I keep reminding myself that this weekend I can sleep in. I am giving myself the mornings off and am going to completely catch up on sleep. Well, sleep and time with Ty. I know the experts all say that catching up on sleep is not healthy or doesn't work. Right now, it's my only option and I'm quite certain, if given the opportunity, I could sleep for twenty-four hours straight. Oh, and I should clarify, by mornings off, I mean I don't have to be at the shop until 9:00 am.

As I walk through the maze of boxes to get to my kitchen, I have to laugh, for if I didn't I would cry for days. My tiny apartment has become the storage unit for my business. Until all of the construction is complete, all of the supplies have been delivered right to my building. I have also managed to not only use up Ty's entire spare bedroom for storage, but I am spilling over into his living space as well. I think it is a good thing the boxes are spread out, otherwise, I just might be overwhelmed. I say that with complete sarcasm. I am overwhelmed; I just don't have time to feel it. As soon as all of these boxes are out of here, I am hiring a housekeeper.

Today is supposed to be the last day of construction. I have reserved the next few days for moving in and my initial product creation. I have managed to rope every one of my loving friends into at least one shift over the next three days. I have bribed them all with my undying love and free chocolate. They are such good people.

I jump out of the shower through on my outfit du jour, jeans, a long sleeve shirt, sneakers and a fleece. I don't even bother with my hair these days, I figure it is just going to end up dust filled and will need a re-wash anyway so why bother! I down a quick cup of joe, grab my wallet, phone, laptop and head to the nearest coffee shop to pick up my morning bribe. I have learned that a paycheck is not as powerful a kick-start as free coffee and donuts in the morning. Of course I will not stop there, these men have been fantastic. I am buying them lunch, and giving them an extra couple hundred cash for each of them if the work gets done today.

As I begin my routine walk down Beacon Street, turning onto Mass Ave heading towards Newbury, I get a funny feeling in my stomach. After today, everything really begins to fall upon me. Up until this point, I have been at the mercy of others, I needed to wait for the right space to become free, wait for the contractors to build it out to my specifications, and wait for the vendors to get all of my supplies in line. After today, there isn't any more relying on others or using them as an excuse for my lack of progress, it all comes down to me. Shit.

I run through the timeline that I have carefully laid out in my head. In many ways, opening a business seems like any other major event. There is a lot of work at the beginning, then there is a bit of a lull, and then, the full on 100 percent push of everything that could not be done until you are down to the wire. My timeline goes something like this:

> Tuesday through Friday: Unpacking, Organizing, finishing touches, and initial product creation.
>
> Saturday: training the new employees (all three of them).
>
> Sunday, September 20th through Friday September 25th: product creation.
>
> Saturday and Sunday: "Gorilla Marketing".
>
> Monday & Tuesday: More product creation.
>
> Wednesday, September 30th: The special invitation party for local concierge, wedding & party planners, and realtors.
>
> Thursday, October 1st: Special guest soft opening.
>
> Friday, October 2nd –: Product creation.
>
> Saturday, October 3, 2015, D Day: The Grand Opening of Truffle This.

I originally thought I would open November 1st. But with careful consideration and research, meaning a chat with my friends, I decided early October would be best. Who knows, it is really just a guess. The actual opening became more dependent on when the construction was going to be complete and the fact that I am not really fond of paying a great deal of rent on a space that is not bringing in any money. Add in all of the startup costs, marketing, website, and supplies; I am bleeding money. If I am not open, not only am I not making any money; I'm not even stopping the bleeding. I need to open.

I leave the coffee shop loaded down with coffees and donuts, my workbag and my city satchel. I loop around down the side street to enter into my storefront from the back alley. The construction paper is staying up on the front facing windows for now. I like the curiosity it seems to be building on Newbury Street as I ease drop on people's conversations about what might be opening soon. As I put down the coffees to dig for my keys I decide that before the end of the day I will buy a coffee maker for the store. I am not going to deal with this juggling act every morning. When I finally find my keys I go to unlock the door and it is open. That is odd. I did not hear the guys inside. I head inside yelling, "Hello."

I do not get any answer. I plop all of my gear on the beautiful countertops and look around. The place looks amazing. They painted the walls it is unbelievable. But there is no sign of anyone. I walk in the back to the kitchen. "Hello."

Again, no answer. I check the stock room and the bathroom, no one. The guys must have left in a hurry last night and forgot to lock the back door. I head back into the front room and I hear something. "Hello?" I call out.

I hear more noise, "Hello?" I call out again, starting to get nervous, I grab my phone.

"Lexi?"

My heartbeat begins to slow down as Paul and Dan, my construction crew, come walking in from the back door.

"Good morning." I say.

"Hey Lexi, what do you think?" Paul asks with a proud smile.

"I think you are both miracle workers and the place looks amazing! Truly!" I respond as I look around again. I can't believe what they have accomplished in two weeks. The walls are painted half pink and chocolate. They are like a sliced open raspberry cream truffle. The display cases are shining and fit perfectly under a custom-made white wooden counter top. The pendant lights are strategically placed throughout the storefront to shed just the right amount of light while adding a flair of funkiness. Once all of the truffles are made it is going to look like candy land for adults.

"Good. I am glad you like it. Well, we will not be here all day. As you can see we were able to finish the painting last night. We are just going to put up all of the hardware and should be done by eleven." Paul states.

"By eleven this morning?" I ask in disbelief.

"Yep."

"Wow. Okay then. I will run back and load my car up and get ready to move things in."

"Sounds good Lex." Paul says as he and Dan dig into the donuts.

I begin to head out; suddenly full of energy as it begins to sink in that the place is going to be mine truly all mine in a matter of hours. I get to the back door and remember the lock and turn around to head back in.

"Hey Paul," I call out, "when I came in this morning the door was open."

Paul gives me a funny look. "What do you mean open?"

"It was unlocked." I respond.

Paul looks at Dan and Dan shakes his head. "We locked it Lexi." Paul and Dan head to the back door to investigate. Paul examines the lock and begins to fiddle with it. He pulls out his key and puts it in the lock and turns it. Nothing happens. He tries again and then asks for my key. He tries my key and nothing.

"Lexi, I think this lock has been picked." Paul states.

"What?" I exclaim.

"Yeah, Lex, someone broke in here. Did you look to see if anything was missing?"

"There isn't anything to steal Paul."

"Well, you have a lot of big equipment in the kitchen." Paul responds.

The three of us quickly head into the kitchen but everything is there; the beautiful Viking range, all of the cold storage, the three industrial mixers, and the Enrober. It is all very expensive but, too large for someone to move without equipment or serious strength. "It is all here." I say as I look back to Paul and Dan.

They nod their heads in agreement. "Lexi, it was probably just curious kids, but regardless, you need to call the police and a lock smith. These locks need to be changed and now you need to start using that fancy alarm system we had installed."

There goes my bubble of joy and happiness. The guys head to work and I head outside to make my calls.

The police arrive quickly as I am on Newbury Street, it's very early, and there are always police in the area. They ask Paul, Dan, and me the typical questions as they look around my storefront and examine all of the entrances. They ask two questions that were unnerving to me. The first was whether there is anyone who may want to harm me or my business, a jilted lover or angry client; and the second was have I noticed anything odd or anyone acting unusual or suspiciously. *Yes, and yes* I thought to myself. But how the heck do I explain a creepy stranger who I saw a few times on the street and who may or may not have been spotted by the singing homeless guy who sits outside the CVS? How do I explain that sometimes I get a chill and I feel like I am being watched? I need the police on my side. I do not need them to think I'm a complete whack job. And as far as jilted lovers well my ex-fiancé of over eight years ago has since gotten married and moved to Alaska, Dominic only cares about what is right in front of him. Nick is not only not jilted he is in Seattle and felt so guilty he placed a $25,000 order. Patrick, although an odd duck, is married. As far as clients, I do not think anyone would want to harm me but who knows.

The only other person who comes to mind is, I shiver, Alistair and he thankfully is locked up in a maximum-security prison. I answered the police officer with a simple "no, not that I can think of."

The police officer told me that whoever did this was not quite an expert; but knew what they were doing. He figured it was probably someone hoping to find more easily removable and expensive items. He told me to do exactly as Paul had suggested, change the locks and utilize my security system. He also told me to be careful at night and not be here too late alone and to never, ever leave here at night with money or make any late night deposits. And his most chilling statement, "Lexi, as a new business owner you need to be vigilant. You are always being watched here on Newbury Street. Unfortunately, you're not always being watched by good people."

I took a deep breath, all joy and happiness has been completely wiped out and replaced with apprehension and fear. "Gees, I just want to make truffles. Since when did chocolate become a dangerous endeavor. I thought the only person I was going to have to keep an eye on was the dude who drives the little Lindt Chocolate car and dresses up in a giant bunny costume."

The Police officer chuckled. "We will keep an eye out Lexi, but you need to be cognizant of who and what is around you. Here is my card, call me anytime, I am usually close by."

"Thank you. And hey, there is always free chocolate right here for Boston's Finest, stop by anytime." I replied. And I meant it. I was planning on making sure I take care of those who watch out for me; after today it is with absolute certainty I will be beyond kind to them.

After the police left Paul and Dan got busy on their work. I had the locksmith coming in a few hours so I took advantage of the time to go home and fill up my car with some of the boxes cluttering up my apartment. I parked my car illegally behind the store and ran up to Crate and Barrel to purchase a new coffee maker. I was determined to not let fear get in the way of my progress. What choice do I have? I am in way too deep financially to let some small break in de-rail all that I have worked so hard for. Break-ins are always going to be a potential. I need to be vigilant, more vigilant, just like the officer told me.

I make it back to my storefront just before ten thirty in the morning. I walk in through the back entrance of the store out into to the front room and find Paul, Dan, Ty and the locksmith having a conversation. Great, just what every girl doesn't need, a circle of testosterone to lecture her on how to stay safe.

I place the coffee maker on the floor and greet them, "Gentlemen."

They all turn and Ty comes over and gives me a big hug. "Yes, Paul and Dan told me everything. Yes, I do think you can handle anything and are one of the strongest women I know. No, I will not be overbearing and over protective. But, yes I do plan on walking you home every night." Ty says as he gives me a look that tells me he has already made his decision and I am going to have to live with it.

I look over to Paul, Dan, and the locksmith they all shrug and nod showing their solidarity with Ty.

"Fine." I say lifting my hands in the air as if to give up. I walk over and introduce myself to the locksmith.

By six in the evening I am exhausted and amazed. Ty and I sit on the floor of my storefront leaning against the wall gulping down water and debating whether to get up or just sleep right where we are. We got so much done. The locksmith changed all of the locks and added some more. The security system has been activated and tested. It even has a camera set up that I can access from my laptop. Yes, I know had it been activated I would have known who tried to break into my store, lesson learned.

We managed to move all of the boxes from my apartment and his into the storefront. All placed exactly where they need to be. My perishable supplies are all being delivered tomorrow, and my friends are coming in the late afternoon to help me decorate. Dare I say, I am ahead of schedule.

Ty takes his last gulp of water and says, "I'm starving."

"Me too. I owe you dinner, what would you like?"

"Take out and a bottle of wine."

"Perfect." I reply.

We still can't move, but if we start thinking about food it may motivate us to get up. Ty hoists himself up off the floor and turns to me and extends his hand to help me up. He pulls me to him, wraps his arms around me and gives me a big hug and a kiss. He whispers, "It is going to be amazing baby doll. And for the record, you owe me nothing!"

"Thank you. You're my hero. I am one lucky girl." I say with a smile and we move to gather my bags and head out to find takeout.

Ty is my hero. Why can't I find a man like Ty? Oh wait, he is my man! I'm still getting used to that.

Ty and I pick up Thai food and a bottle of red wine and walk back to his place. My place is a disaster and I haven't done laundry in two weeks. Thankfully I do have a drawer full of clean clothes at Ty's place. The only reason I have clean clothes at his house is because he took pictures of a bunch of my clothes and then sent his assistant out to buy similar items to keep at his house. I am normally not such a mess but opening a storefront is a bigger undertaking than I could have ever predicted. And Ty, well, he is just a saint. Ty plates our take out, pours the wine and we snuggle up on the couch to enjoy our casual dine in.

"How are you doing?" Ty asks in between bites.

"You're going to have to be more specific love. I'm not sure where to begin to answer that question." I laugh as I shove an overloaded fork full of Pad Thai into my mouth.

"How are you with this break-in situation?" Ty asks rather seriously.

Ty is a saint and one that I am lying to. Lying to a saint, I'm quite certain puts me on the fast track to hell. I chew slowly so I can ponder my response. The truth is I am completely freaked out but I don't want to think about it because I can't slow down. To be totally honest I thought about shutting the whole thing down when we figured out someone had broken in. I don't want my store to be robbed or to be held up at gunpoint when depositing money. I don't want to be scared every morning when I go to work and then every night when

I come home. I'm freaked out, but all of my money is tied up in this, all of the work, my life, I can't afford to be scared. "I'm fine. We put the right systems in place, I feel good about things." I finally respond.

"Lexi, look at me and say that."

I couldn't look at him. I pretended to be focused on the food, even though my stomach was beginning to turn.

"Lexi." Ty said sternly. Clearly he was not buying into my bullshit.

I put my fork down and took a swig of wine. "Okay, but you can't get mad."

Ty just tilted his head and raised an eyebrow at me.

"There is more to the story." I began and waited to measure his reaction through his body language. Ty leaned back against the couch and told me to proceed. Yep, he's pissed.

"Ty I have been meaning to tell you things, but, I, we have both been so insanely busy, I just keep forgetting. I mean, when we are together and we are both actually awake, I don't want to talk about the bad stuff. I just want to snuggle up to you, and kiss you, and rip your clothes off and have crazy, amazing sex." I end my justification with little pouty eyes.

"What bad stuff?" Ty asks more concerned than stern this time.

Damn it. There is no avoiding this. "Some odd things have happened this summer. Initially, I thought I was just stressed and perhaps a bit paranoid. They happened occasionally and I didn't really put things together. I thought if I said anything you'd think I was nuts. But now, with the break-in maybe it's more than stress. Or not, I don't know." I stop to gage Ty's reactions. The last time I told him something crazy he disappeared for a week. I know circumstances are completely different now, but I am still fearful.

"Lexi, you have had some insane things happen in your life. Real things, that are insane. If you're sensing something, with all that has gone on in your life, I'm believing you."

My heart is now beating in my chest as if it is trying to pound its way out. "Right. I'm trying to remember back to all of the instances that have happened. My head is so overstuffed with information."

"Take your time." Ty says as he rubs his hand over my knee.

His touch calms me. "It was this summer, June maybe. I had just had lunch with my friends and as I was leaving Stephanie's I got this weird feeling and I saw this guy and it was if time slowed down and we starred at each other. It happened really quickly and then he was gone. I think I saw the guy again standing on the Mass Ave Bridge. And there were a couple of other times that I just got a feeling like I was being watched. I can't really explain it." I stop to think. "Oh and then the singing homeless guy who sits outside of CVS, you know him?"

"Yeah." Ty says completely bewildered.

"So, I saw the guy again, the one from outside Stephanie's and I was across the street from CVS and he disappeared again. And then the homeless guy started singing to me that I was a girl who just saw a ghost."

"Ok, but he probably just noticed the look on your face."

"Right." I stop and take a sip of wine. My mind is now on warp speed. "But then sometime later, weeks, days, I'm not sure. He sings to me again. He sings something about my ghost; that my ghost was there. And then he did it again, and said to my left and I saw the guy. He ducked down an alley and I ran after him."

"You did what?" Ty loudly interrupts.

"I know, it wasn't the smartest move, but I just reacted. He was gone."

"Lexi, I don't know where to start. Why haven't you told me any of this?" Ty stands up and begins to pace around the living room.

"I don't know, I guess, I thought I was being paranoid. And I was just anxious with everything going on and not talking about Ashley and Alistair and all that happened. I thought that because of the stress my mind was playing tricks on me. I was scared and I didn't want to be. So, if I didn't talk about it and just forgot about it, it wasn't real. Until maybe now."

"Until now." Ty nods his head in agreement. "Do you have any idea who this guy could be?"

"No. It could be no one. I mean it's been awhile since any siting's or creepy feelings have happened."

"But now, your storefront was broken into." Ty says.

"Yes."

"Anything else odd you need to tell me?"

I shake my head no. "Well, maybe. So remember that odd duck Patrick?"

"Yes." Ty says slowly as he sits back down on the coach.

"Well, I told you he is married and I ran into him and his wife. He introduced us. She seemed nice. Anyway, the night you came over, that first night?"

"Mm hmm." Ty moans with a half sexy grin.

"Well, I was about to call the police when you were knocking on the door. Patrick was out on the street screaming my name and I looked out the window and he was completely hammered. He just stood there, well tried to stand there yelling my name and I didn't know what to do so I was going to call the cops. How did you not hear him?"

Ty thinks for a moment. "I was downstairs for a bit talking to Tom, but we were down the hall away from the front door. I must have come into the building before he started yelling. Did you tell any of this to the police?"

"No. And before you ask, I don't know why. I guess I don't want any more crazy Ty. I just want to make truffles. And, I do not want to be the paranoid, crazy store owner that they roll their eyes about."

"I am going to ask you to do something. Well, I am going to ask, just so I sound nice. If I am completely honest, it is not a question you can say no to. I want you to stay here."

"Tonight?" I ask, slightly confused as I was already planning on it.

"Indefinitely." Ty says.

I was too tired to argue. And if I really thought about it I was too relieved to argue.

17

My alarm goes off at 5:30 in the morning. Ty reaches over me, turns it off, slides one arm underneath me and one over my waist creating the perfect spoon and my perfect cocoon. There is nothing better than waking up next to Ty every morning. There is also nothing more difficult than trying to leave his bed every morning. We have been living in the same space for two weeks now and it's so seamless it feels as though we have been living together for years. I finally roll out of bed, ignoring Ty's groans, and jump into the shower.

I exit the bedroom all showered and packed. I am wearing my usual jeans and a fleece but I have packed a bag with a dress and high-heeled knee length boots for tonight's festivities. I can't believe we are having the soft opening tonight. Yesterday was an invited-guest party for realtors, concierge, event and wedding planners; basically anyone who would potentially refer me customers and hopefully become a customer themselves. It seemed as though everyone was enjoying themselves, now I just need the orders and customers to start trickling in. I walk into the kitchen and Ty is standing there in his pajama bottoms, no shirt and two piping hot cups of coffee in his hands. I don't think I will ever get tired of seeing that every morning.

"Are you trying to torture me?" I jest.

Ty flashes me my favorite smile. "If I thought I had a shot of keeping you in bed all to myself, I wouldn't have put on pants."

"You're evil."

"I checked my email while you were in the shower. You are getting rave reviews!"

"I am? That's great!" I say as I take a quick sip of coffee and reach for my phone. As I scroll through my emails I see orders. Actual orders from yesterday's event. "Holy cow Ty, I have orders!"

Ty grabs my phone, "Seriously?" He scrolls through and the smile on his face just gets bigger. "Lexi, this is unbelievable! Look at them all!" Ty puts my phone on the counter and scoops me up and spins me around the room. "I had no doubt, I just didn't think it would be so quick." He whispers.

"Right!" I exclaim. Suddenly it dawns on me I have to make all of the truffles to fill these orders all the while producing product for tonight's soft opening and my grand opening on Saturday. A rush of panic comes over me.

Ty notices my face change. "Lexi, it's all right. This is good. Just set Saint Sally up on your laptop and have her start logging all of the orders by date needed. She is a whiz, you said so yourself. Let's not panic before you actually know what is in front of you. Just focus on tonight. I'm here. I can do any running around, waiting on customers, anything you need."

"How did I ever get so lucky?" I say as I kiss Ty.

"We both got lucky Lexi. I just finally get to pay you back for all of those years of backing me off the ledge. Now you get to lean on me. And I want you to." Ty gives me a kiss. "Now go, you've got work to do girl. I will be there by three this afternoon."

I kiss Ty and head out the door. I walk up to Newbury Street smiling the whole way. This is my life. This is actually my life. I get to take this walk every day. I have a storefront on Newbury Street. I have a man who is the most amazing man a girl could ever want. And I have sales. I have friggin' sales! *Thank you Universe!*

I unlock the door to my storefront and quickly deactivate the alarm. I lock the door behind me, as my team is not showing up until noon today. The soft opening party is from five thirty in the evening until seven thirty with about fifty guests expected. Fifty is really the maximum I could fit into my store at one time. The guest list consists of my closest friends, some friends of Ty's who did not make it to the party yesterday, a few key players and business owners from the Back Bay neighborhood, and some contacts of Ty's from the press who he knows will show their love in the papers and on the radio. Most of the product for tonight is already made. At this point I am focusing on the product for the weekend. I have no idea how many people to expect to stroll into the shop on opening weekend, but I want my display cases full of truffles and my cold storage completely stuffed with product.

This morning my sole focus is on caramel. For me this is the most painstaking product because it is a process you just can't speed up. The sugar melts at a slow pace, if you try and make it melt faster by turning up the heat too quickly; it burns. The butter needs to be added bit by bit. The evaporated milk needs to be stirred in very slowly. The whole time you need to stir and slowly bring the entire mixture up to the perfect temperature so the caramel is hard enough to work with but still soft and chewy. It takes about two hours per batch no matter what. Then I have to let it sit in the cool fridge for about two hours before I am able to cut it and coat it in chocolate. I have learned to live with the time it takes to make the caramel, because the result is just a mouth full of perfectly sweet and buttery goodness.

By eleven in the morning I managed to complete two batches of caramel and have them both cooling before being cut and coated. I have enough time to head to Deluca's market and pick up lunch for my team and me before they arrive. I lock the door behind me but I do not bother setting the alarm. It is the middle of the day; I do not see the need for extra security. My windows are still covered in construction paper but now the paper has huge print reading: *Truffle This Grand Opening Saturday, October 3rd!*

I reach the crowded corner of Newbury and Fairfield. Deluca's is across Newbury Street and the CVS is across Fairfield to my right and I hear; "No ghosts today ghost hunter, how about some money ghost hunter." I'm not sure how he saw me with everyone standing on the corner, but my singing homeless guy seems to see everything. I ignore him and cross over to Deluca's market. I am done chasing ghosts. Alistair is locked up for good. I haven't seen delusional Patrick in quite some time and I haven't seen my ghost either.

I leave Deluca's with two bags full of sandwiches, chips and waters. I cross Newbury Street and hand the singing homeless guy a water and put a dollar in his coffee can. He didn't sing to me but he actually looked at me and said "Thank you, no ghosts." That gave me a bigger chill than anything else. I would love to come back and give him a big box of chocolates, but with my luck he has diabetes and I would accidentally put my favorite homeless guy into a diabetic coma. I figured water and money is my safest bet.

I get to my storefront door and between stirring caramel for four hours and lugging two heavy bags a block and a half my arms feel like they are going to fall off. I put the bags down to unlock the doors and I hear, "Boo!" I jumped five feet in the air.

"Oh, Lexi, I'm so sorry I didn't mean to scare you!" said Paul.

I catch my breath and realize it is my new employee Paul, showing up for work. Clearly I'm not quite over my ghost angst. "Paul, no it's fine. Great to see you on this exciting day!"

"That it is Lexi. Here let me help with those bags." Paul says as he grabs the sandwich filled bags off the sidewalk.

Paul has turned out to be a lucky hire. Not only did he go to culinary school, he has a particular interest in confections. He also has a great deal of experience working an Enrober machine. I'm learning more from him than he is from me. And he is a worker. He is fast and flawless in his efforts.

Saint Sally and Regina walk into the store shortly after Paul and myself. I set Sally up right away on the laptop to start sifting through all of the orders I received yesterday. Regina is another lucky hire.

She is an art major at Boston University with a lot of retail experience. I hired her because of her retail experience; little did I know how valuable her artistic mind would be. My storefront looks like it was completed by one of the top interior designers in the country. It is exquisite and it is all Regina! When thinking about all of the time that went into sorting through hundreds of emails and resumes, and sitting through tortured interviews, I realize it was all worth it. I have the trifecta! Now I just have to hang onto this trifecta!

By five in the evening my storefront and my team are ready for the soft opening.

I hired a catering company to handle the drinks and the food. All of the food is to be passed on trays consisting mostly of cheese, fruit, and bread; flavors that pair well with chocolate. The chocolate is also being passed on trays by my team versus just displayed on a buffet table. We decided that was the best option to avoid any chocolate getting too soft. Even with it being a cool October evening a room filled with fifty people can quickly become quite warm.

The construction paper covering the windows has been removed and stored to be put back up at the end of the night. I still have to create product tomorrow and I will not want people erroneously thinking I am open. A red carpet has been placed in front of the store doors with a big backdrop reading *Truffle This* so guests can have their pictures taken Hollywood style. This of course was all Regina's idea. She enlisted one of her classmates to take photos to use for the website and any future PR. Paul recruited two of his friends to wear suits and stand guard at the door while checking to be sure guests were on the list. Young people have the best energy! And boy did their ideas work! As guests started to arrive we had quite the crowd of onlookers. The red carpet, two young men in suits, and flash from the camera created quite a scene. I decided to send Regina and Sally out onto the street with trays of chocolates and grand opening notification cards for the curious crowds of people. It worked. Four times in a span of thirty minutes they each came back inside to restock their trays.

The event was turning out to be quite something. My friends were indulging in chocolate and champagne. Ty was working the room in between interrogations by my friends on our relationship status. The conversations seemed to be less about our relationship and more about why it took us so long to finally cross over the friend line. Ty would occasionally give me a wink during his conversations with my friends to let me know he was just fine. I never doubted he would be any other way. I step into the kitchen doorway and take a look at the storefront. I am still in awe that this is all happening.

"Excuse me Lexi." Paul interrupts my moment of soaking it all in.

"Yes, sir, what can I do for you?" I ask. Even though Truffle This is technically my business, there is no doubt in my mind that Paul's experience and knowledge far surpasses mine and he is really in charge tonight.

Paul smiles. "My friends out front just informed me that there is a couple at the door who are not on the list but say they are friends of yours."

"Really? Hmm, I will go check it out. Thanks Paul."

As I make my way across the room towards the door Ty manages to disengage himself from my friends and intercept me before I reach the door.

"Where have you been all my life?" Ty asks as he pulls me towards him with one hand and hands me a glass of champagne with his other.

I smile and reach up to give him a kiss. "Right here." I respond. "But, I have to head outside, apparently someone knows me but is not on the list."

"Uh-oh, did you make a faux pas already?" Ty asks in jest.

"Apparently." I say smiling.

Ty follows me outside. Standing off to the side is Patrick and his wife. I could not believe my eyes. This man is preposterous! "Who's that?" Ty whispers.

"Patrick and his wife."

"You're kidding me." Ty says still keeping his voice to a whisper.

"Should I just let him in? I don't want a scene." I ask Ty.

Ty looks over at Patrick and his wife and shakes his head. "Yeah, you might as well. I'll keep an eye on him."

As I walk over to Patrick and his wife I decide quickly that they are not coming in. He is crazy and I am done with all insanity in my life. "Hi." I say not really hiding my bewilderment.

"Lexi, hi." Patrick responds. "I guess we're not on the list."

"Well, it is really a party for my closest friends. The grand opening is Saturday."

"We are sorry Lexi. We will come back on Saturday when it's more appropriate. Go enjoy your friends." Patrick's wife responds looking utterly embarrassed.

"Thanks Karen. I'm really sorry, I'm at my maximum of allowable people inside." I respond, grateful that she is seemingly normal.

"We totally get it, go enjoy." Karen says as she leads Patrick away from my storefront.

"Well done Lex. Crisis averted." Ty says as he reaches for my hand and leads me back inside.

"I think you mean "crazy" averted." I joked.

By nine thirty that evening everything was quiet. My amazing team of young people had packed up and gone home. The caterers had cleaned up leaving us a tray of fruit and cheese and a bottle of champagne. The construction paper was back up on the front windows. By the time we arrived back at Ty's place after locking everything up and setting the alarm we were so exhausted we both collapsed into bed.

18

A WAKE UP

I slipped out of bed before my alarm went off. I slept from ten in the evening until six thirty this morning. Eight and a half hours of solid sleep was much needed. I could keep sleeping but I have to get started on my day. All I have is a wake up and Truffle This will be open. I decide to forgo the shower and grab coffee on Newbury Street. Ty looks so peaceful sleeping that I don't want to do anything to wake him up. Paul, Saint Sally, and Regina are all due in by noon today so I can slip home and shower then. Right now I'm feeling quite rested and want to get a jumpstart on my day.

I quietly close the door to Ty's apartment. I then check my purse and my laptop bag to be sure I have everything I need, specifically my keys. I exit the brownstone and shutter at the sharpness of the cold air on my lungs. It is freezing this morning and I am not exactly dressed for it. I pop into Starbucks to get a banana and some coffee. I am not sure what we have left for coffee supplies after last evening. And although I'm feeling rather well rested this morning, it doesn't change the fact that I am not a morning person. I need my coffee and I need it now.

I arrive at my storefront and quickly unlock the back door and hustle inside. My hands are so cold I can barely punch in the code to deactivate the alarm. I throw my things down and pull out my laptop and fire it up. I pull up a comfortable chair and begin scanning the morning news. Even though I am at my place of business, I still need to ease into my day. I need to sip my coffee and quickly review any important news headlines and then linger a little longer on the more entertaining gossipy websites. I click over to the MSN lifestyle section to peruse the 5 to 7 ways I should be doing everything. I always get a kick out of the headlines. There are always five, seven, or ten ways I should be doing something. This morning is particularly funny. The first headline reads: *5 Ways to Kill a Relationship*. Why would you want to kill it? Just leave. Right underneath that headline is the *7 Ways to be Better in Bed*. That one I should probably read later. Ty and I have great sex; but I am always open to suggestions on improving my game. And lastly, *10 Surprising Uses for Lemons*. Where do they come up with this stuff? With all of the information that is on the Internet these days it has to be getting harder to be original.

I finally stop wasting time and decide to get down to business. How much time do you think the average American wastes on the Internet? I'm very tempted to Google that question but I resist. And when did Google become a noun and a verb? I have to focus. I am procrastinating. I am a bit scared to look at the order sheet Saint Sally completed yesterday. She said I would be very happy with the results. Little does she know I actually need to be extremely happy. I went through my finances the other day and realized that I have about enough money to make it for another two months. I need to start making money and fast. The only back up money I have is my retirement and credit cards, neither of which would ever be recommended to be used as back up by anyone with any financial wherewithal. Actually, most financial advisors would have told me to save up another six months of expenses. I thought I had plenty in the bank; but starting a business is very expensive. If I were to offer any new business owner advice, I would say to not only have one year's worth of living expenses; but to take your estimated start-up costs and triple them.

I pull open Saint Sally's spreadsheet. I am scared to look. I begin to scroll down and there are a lot of orders. I look at the bottom and

I can't believe it. I seriously can't believe it. We have twenty thousand dollars' worth of orders. I double-check her formula set up to be sure it is accurate. It is of course. I breathe a heavy sigh of relief. *Thank you Universe.* I'm astonished, relieved, and elated. I think I just got five years added back to my life. Trying to figure out how to get these orders filled and shipped or delivered on time, well that will take those five years back off my life; but for now, I feel relief, just pure sweet relief.

I finish my coffee and decide to get to work. I need to figure out what we have left for inventory and start replenishing our truffles. I want to get the most painstaking ones done first. I have always been told, and find it to be true, if you get the hardest or most dreaded task done first, the rest of your day seems so much easier.

I am banging around in my kitchen trying to get set up for the day and I feel a chill. I hope I am not coming down with something. It has been a lot of long days and stress and walking to my storefront this morning underdressed in the freezing cold was not one of my smartest moves. I need to text Ty and ask him to bring me some emergen-C when he goes to work. Better safe than sorry. I can't find my phone anywhere. I head into the front room to find my purse. The front room is feeling exceptionally chilly to me and I realize I did not lock the back door. I need to lock it to keep it from opening and letting all of the cold air in. I find my phone and shove it in my back pocket. I spin around and am silenced by what I see.

I think I may be sick. I slowly raise my hands. I step back even more slowly. I can't take my eyes off the gun.

"Good morning Lexi."

I don't know what to think or say or do. This can't be happening. Is that a real gun? "What are you doing?" I ask.

"Well, I am not here to rob you if that is what you're worried about."

That was not at all what I was worried about. I am however freaked the hell out that I am looking at a gun.

"Sit down Lexi. We need to have a talk."

"A talk?" I ask slowly backing towards the chair.

"Yes, a talk. A talk about my husband, Patrick. I think you know him."

A talk. Karen wants to have a talk about her husband while she is pointing a gun at me. I will myself to calm down. A talk means a chance. I might have a chance. I need to remember every little thing I know about human behavior right now. Holy shit I am scared. My heart is beating so fast and so hard I can feel it against my chest. I am either going to puke or pass out. I can feel the adrenaline beginning to flood my body. "All right." I say as I delicately slide into the chair.

Karen never takes the gun off me. "Have you ever been married Lexi?"

"No." I quietly respond.

"Do you understand what it means to be married to someone Lexi? Do you understand the meaning of marriage?" Karen is now very condescending in her tone. She clearly has a message to deliver.

"I believe I do yes." I respond, saying as little as possible right now as I don't want to make a mistake with my words.

"Huh, I find that interesting. You see Lexi; most people who understand marriage would not try and steal someone else's husband. I mean I can understand why you would go after my husband. But he is MINE." She got very loud while stressing the word mine.

Her eyes got crazy with rage and I assume jealousy. She stared at me in a way that if her eyes could pull the trigger; I would be dead. I've seen this look before in other people, the difference being they weren't holding a gun. She is irrational. I can't fight crazy. I can't reason with crazy. I don't know if she is just threatening me or if she would actually pull the trigger. I can't tell. "I'm, uh, I, um, I'm not after your husband Karen." I stutter.

"Really? So now he's not good enough for you, is that it? You went on two dates with him." Karen sarcastically responds.

"I did. But, he told me you were divorced, and the…"

"So now my husband is a LIAR?" Karen screams as she interrupts me mid-sentence.

Oh God my stomach is churning. "No, I did not say that. Your husband, when I met him, said he was divorced and then after the second date, for which I am very sorry, he told me he was married. And that was it Karen, I did not go out with him again. I swear." I am clasping my hands on my knees as I beg for some form of rational thought from her.

"Really? That is interesting to hear Lexi." Karen says in an eerily calm voice. The voice one gets right before they are about to explode.

"It's true Karen." I say watching her as she paces back and forth.

Karen reaches in to her pocket and I stop breathing. I let out a shallow breath when she pulls a phone out of her pocket.

"Tell me Lexi," Karen begins still using her overly calm voice, "why then have you been constantly texting my husband?"

"What?" I can't hide my utter confusion.

"These!" Karen screams as she shoves the phone in my face.

I look at the phone. "May I?"

Karen hands me the phone and I scroll through the messages. My hands are shaking so badly I can barely read the screen. They are long rambling text messages saying I love him. They have my name next to them. He responds with things like, "leave me alone, I'm married." These are totally false. I look up at her, "Karen, I didn't send these." I say feeling completely defeated. I'm screwed. I feel the tears beginning to well up in my eyes. I can't fight crazy and I certainly can't fight two crazy people.

"You expect me to believe you?" She is calmer. She must sense my utter defeat and this has somehow softened her a bit. Her eyes seem more normal, more human.

"I swear Karen; I did not send those." I say, still holding back my tears.

Karen for the first time stops pointing the gun at me and lets her hand drop to her side. She paces more slowly, more contemplative, almost rational. Suddenly there is a loud knock at the front door. Karen quickly spins around pointing the gun at me and shaking her head, signaling me not to say a word. My body stiffens as I sit straight and clench the bottom of the chair with both hands. *Please don't be Ty, please no. The people I love die and I survive.* I pray to myself it is not Ty. Another loud knock and "UPS" the man behind the door shouts.

My shoulders relax a bit with the relief; but my hands hold their firm grip on the seat. Karen stands straight holding the gun pointed between the door and me. After one more knock and shout from the UPS driver, we stay in our respective stances for what feels like forever. Silence.

Karen begins to pace again, a bit more chaotic now. She looks like she is talking to herself. Her pace is too fast, she got scared and I have lost the rational side of her. She stops and just stares at me. "Did you kiss him?" She asks, her voice back to the eerily calm tone.

Oh God how do I answer this?

"DID YOU KISS HIM?" She screams at me while motioning the gun at me to accent every word.

I'm shaking. I have never been so scared. I can't breathe. I feel the blood leaving my face.

"ANSWER ME!" She screams.

Maybe if I tell her the truth, maybe she will calm down, maybe she just wants an answer. Time, I need time. "No." I barely whisper.

"What? No." Karen looks at me confused but still holding the gun pointed at me.

I gain some strength and conviction. I look her in the eye, "no."

She just stares at me. And then a clanking noise comes from the back. We both quickly look in the direction of the back door.

"What was that?" Karen asks as she is pointing the gun towards the back.

"I don't know."

"I locked the door. Who has a key?" She asks.

My mind races to Ty. Please no, not Ty. "No one. It is probably a mouse." I respond.

"Clank, clank." We hear it again.

"Did you say a mouse?" Karen asks her voice very shaky at this point.

She seems frightened. Really frightened. I realize the girl holding a gun is afraid of mice. "Yes, we saw one the other night." I lie.

Karen looks at me with complete fear. The color is gone from her face and she is pale. She has a fear of mice. Fear is funny that way it can take away all sense of reason and power. She has a gun, what the hell is a mouse going to do to her? It doesn't matter. I have to use this. Think Lexi, think.

"Karen." A man's voice calls from the back.

Karen quickly turns towards the voice then back to me. Her eyebrows are raised and her eyes wide but angry. She turns herself away from me and towards the back of the storefront pointing the gun haphazardly in the direction of the back hall. A man slowly appears with his hands up just above his waist.

"Who the hell are you? Don't move." Karen screeches like a scared child, as she steady's her stance a bit.

I struggle to see the man's face as he steps into the light very slowly.

Karen looks to me still pointing the gun in the direction of the man. "Who is he?" she screams.

"I, I don't..." I stop mid-sentence. Holy shit, it's him. My fear and disbelief rise to a level I didn't know existed. I'm going to pass out.

"Don't Move." Karen demands as she points the gun more directly at him. "Who is he?" She yells in my direction.

"I don't know." I whisper. But I do.

"Don't move or I will shoot you. I WILL!" Karen shoves the gun through the air towards the ghost.

"Karen, you're not going to shoot anyone. Besides, the police are on their way. They are probably right outside the door." The ghost says, his voice calm yet firm.

Karen looks behind her to the front door and then down at me. She is shifting from side to side. She's clearly scared. She looks back to the ghost. "Who are you?"

"Karen my name is Richard. Now can we talk? Without the gun?" Richard asks in a stronger more commanding voice.

Richard? I'm so confused.

"Karen," Richard continues, "you are clearly very upset and with good reason. However, I am not the one you are mad at." He pauses to measure Karen's response. "And, well, if you really think about it Karen, Lexi is not the one you are mad at either."

Karen is silent for a moment. "Don't tell me who I am mad at." She sternly replies.

"I'm not telling you. I'm sorry. But aren't you really pissed off at your husband? I mean, isn't he the one who has created this mess?" Richard asks rather provocatively.

"No." Karen says as she tries to maintain her stance. "No, Patrick did nothing wrong. People come after him. People like her." Karen turns to me and points the gun in my direction. "Her."

I clench the chair. My eyes never leave the gun. She is so wobbly and shaky it could go off at any second.

"Karen. Think about it. Patrick is a grown man. He makes decisions too. And Lexi, well, Lexi is in love with someone else. She lives with him." Richard is talking to her like she is a five-year-old.

"You are?" Karen looks at me, lowers the gun and her face softens.

"Yes." I respond. *Who the hell is this guy?*

"Karen, the police are right outside. How about you just hand over the gun and we all walk out of here?" Richard asks Karen in a very kind and calm voice.

Karen looks at me. Her eyes now carry a dazed blank stare. Richard has his hand out to Karen and she eventually hands him the gun. Richard extends his other hand to Karen and says, "Come on." Karen takes hold of his hand and Richard leads her out the back door. I stay in the chair, my hands still clenching the seat. I sit for what seems like an eternity. My mind is racing but my body immobile.

"Lexi!" Ty yells as he races through the back door. Two police officers are following closely behind him. "Lexi," Ty says his voice expressing complete relief when he sees me. He kneels down in front of me and wraps his arms around me. I feel his touch, my hands still gripping the seat. I can't move.

"How did you know I was here?"

"Where else would you be Lex?"

"How did you know I was in trouble?"

Ty hugs me more tightly. "Newbury Street is not that big Lexi. I'm right up the road remember?"

I release my hands and wrap them around Ty; only then am I able to release my tears.

19

MY GHOST

I'm not sure I could ever truly convey the utter fear that pulses through your body when staring at a gun. You are present and thoughts are racing through your mind but yet; you leave your body. It's like you are watching something happen to you. Your state of arousal is so high that you float between watching and feeling the fear. I would say the aftermath is even worse but it's not because you are alive. I am alive. Logically there is no better outcome and I know that. But for the immediate hours following the incident I felt numb and limp. I listened to people but I did not comprehend things. I got sick a few times. I was shaky. I was scared.

Karen had a nervous breakdown and was being held at a psychiatric facility. I hope she gets better. I'm not sure where Patrick is but I can tell you he is dangerous. He should be the one locked up. He created the emotional turmoil that Karen was feeling. He is one messed up person.

My shop was run mostly by the amazing team I had in place. I showed up, I made truffles, but that was about as much as I could do. After seeing a trauma specialist every day for two weeks, I was finally ready to sit down with this man named Richard. My ghost who freaked me out all summer and then ended up saving my life. He gave me his card immediately following the incident and said to call when I was ready. I was ready. He is the missing piece to this crazy puzzle. Richard agreed to meet me at Ty's office. I wasn't about to do anything without my pillar of strength, Ty.

When Richard walked into Ty's office my heart began to race. I felt as though I was catapulted back to that day in my storefront. I knew this could happen. I just didn't know it would feel so real. Richard greeted Ty with a handshake and then looked over to me.

"Lexi, hi. Richard Johnston. It's nice to formally meet you."

"Hi Richard." I say as I shake his hand. "Thank you for saving my life."

Richard smiles. "You are quite welcome. I guess now you are wondering who the hell I am and why I was even there."

I nod. We all sit down at Ty's conference table. Richard pulls out a folder with the name A. Morgan written across the top.

"How do you know Ashley?" I ask.

"I don't. But I know the people who run her estate." Richard continues. "Lexi, Ty, I am a former secret service agent turned private investigator. I was hired by the firm that manages Ashley's estate to investigate you Lexi.

"Why me?" I am completely confused.

"Well, because she left you all of her money. And it's a lot of money."

"What?"

"Let me back up. Alistair, as you know, is a very evil and calculating man. He chose Ashley. He had a plan all along and that was to get Ashley's money."

"I know she had a trust fund, but I didn't think it was that big, I mean, seriously, he killed her for what less than a million."

"Well, no. She had two funds. She had the one she was living on, but then she had a much bigger one that she was going to gain access to when she turned 40. She knew this. She was very involved with her finances and very responsible. Alistair also knew this."

"How? Did she tell him?"

"Well, she may have, but Alistair was a fired attorney from the firm managing Ashley's trust fund. He was not on her account; however, he knew who she was and what she had. They have records of him accessing her information before he was fired. That is actually why he was fired."

"So, he sought her out?"

"Yes."

I look over to Ty whose eyes are as wide as mine.

Richard continues, "When Ashley let the firm know that Alistair was going to be her new attorney in Los Angeles the firm went crazy. They sent him notification of legal action and let Ashley know who he was and how fraudulent his actions were. That is when things went very wrong. Alistair panicked and well…"

"He killed Ashley." I interrupted Richard.

"The firm was fine with Ashley naming you as her benefactor when she did; but, as you can imagine after everything that happened, well, they just wanted to be sure you were not involved."

"So they hired you to be certain." Ty pipes in.

"Yes."

"But, how did you know about Karen? How did you know to be there?"

"I can't give you all of my secrets Lexi. I will say this; it was me you saw in the window across from your building."

"Oh my god, I thought I was going crazy."

"I know and I'm sorry about that. You have a much greater sense of awareness than most people. Usually I'm never detected. You were a challenge. Anyway, that night that Patrick was drunk outside of your building, that was a big red flag for me so I started paying closer attention to him."

"How? Did you follow him too?" I ask.

"Secrets Lexi, again, I can't give them all away. Honestly, I was surprised when I saw that Karen was in your storefront, I thought it would have been Patrick."

"How did you see her?"

Richard nods his head toward the ceiling

"You had a camera in my store?"

"I did."

"I want to be angry and say I am feeling violated but, then, you, saved my life."

"Well, I understand. I did violate your privacy and for that I'm sorry.

"So, what now?" I ask.

"Well, you'll be contacted by the firm, here is their information." Richard pulls out a smaller folder and slides it across the table to me. "You are now about twenty million dollars richer. Congratulations and don't talk to strangers."

"Did you say twenty million?" I am having a hard time registering this number.

"I did. And with that, I have a plane to catch."

"Wait, you're leaving, that is it. But, what if I need something or I want to thank you, bigger. I want to thank you in a bigger way. I mean you saved my life." I am sitting on the edge of my seat. I'm not sure I'm ready to let him go.

"Lexi, there is no need. You have thanked me. I was doing my job." Richard stands up and places the folder labeled A. Morgan into his briefcase. He shakes Ty's hand and steps back and looks at both of us. "You know, I'm really happy you two are together. I was rooting for this." Richard motions his hands towards Ty and I.

"What if I need to reach you?" I was suddenly fearful of watching Richard walk away.

"Well, Nick always knows where I am."

"It was you in the picture. I knew it."

Richard laughs. "Well, take care of each other you two. And stay away from strangers Lexi!"

"I can't promise that. Strangers typically turn out to be significant blessings in my life." I smile and give Ty a wink. "But I can promise you that I will stop chasing ghosts."

Richard smiles. I reach out and hug him. I hug my ghost farewell; it was the least I could do.

Made in the USA
Middletown, DE
29 February 2016